HAWKE

SMOKEJUMPERS

BOOK ONE

BY EVIE RILEY

Hawke

Smokejumpers

Book One

Copyright © 2023

Evie Riley

Second Edition

ISBN: 978-1-77357-677-0

Published by Naughty Nights Press LLC

Cover Art By Willsin Rowe

HAWKE

Come on, baby, light my fire...

Firefighter Hawke Colton loves his job and hanging with his firefighter brothers. Work is great, but Hawke wants more. He yearns for a life with a husband, kids, a house, even a dog. What he craves is a real family, something he never got to experience growing up.

Fire Investigator Tristan Cole lost his parents to an arsonist twenty-one years ago. That tragedy changed his life forever. He's built his career on putting arsonists away, and he is still searching for the person responsible for his parents' death.

When a family is killed in a suspicious fire, Tristan knows the signature of the offender all too well. To prove it's the same arsonist, he asks Hawke for help combing through the old files. He is determined to get justice by uncovering what lurks beneath the ashes.

When the arsonist sets his sights on Tristan, can Hawke find a way to keep his new love safe?

CHAPTER ONE

Twenty-One Years Ago...

Tristan

A HIGH PITCH beeping sound brought me out of my sleep. I knew based on how tired I was that it couldn't be my alarm. It was nowhere near time for me to get up for school. Usually, if my alarm was going off, it would turn off after a minute, but this alarm was going strong and not showing any signs of turning off. It also didn't sound like my alarm. It was a sound I'd never heard before, though.

I let out a groan, knowing I would have to go and figure out what it was. If it was still going off then that meant my parents hadn't heard it.

A coughing fit overtook me, my whole body shaking with the force of my coughs. I had no idea what had caused me to start coughing like I was, but that answer came when I opened my eyes to grab my water from the sidetable next to my bed.

My whole room was filled with the dark grey haze of smoke.

Panic started to flood my entire body as I fought for breath. Every single breath felt like sharp knives were slicing me from the inside out. I couldn't stop coughing, no matter how hard I tried, and the more I coughed, the harder it got to breathe. My eyes were starting to burn from the smoke and I knew I had to get out of there. I didn't know where the fire had started, but I knew I couldn't stay in my room.

I forced my body to move, to get out of my bed. I didn't crawl. I knew I was supposed to, but the smoke was so thick, I was afraid I wouldn't be able to find the door.

I ran my hand along the edge of my bed until I reached the end and then I stumbled, reaching out for my dresser that was next to my door. The second my hand touched it, I felt along the edge until finally, I was able to feel my door.

It was hot.

I knew that meant there was a fire

outside of my door, most likely the hallway carpet, but I also knew I definitely couldn't stay in my room. My room was on the third floor, so even if I could get my window opened enough for me to fit through, I couldn't jump. I was too high up. Plus, I couldn't let my parents risk their lives coming upstairs to get me only for me to not be there. The best thing I could do would be to find a way down the stairs and get to my parents.

With more courage than I was feeling, I opened the door and was greeted by fire everywhere. It was on the floor, the walls, and even the ceiling. The whole house was on fire, and for a moment I thought I was trapped. I thought I was going to die in my room, unable to escape. The smoke was just as thick out in the hall, but the light from the fire at least made it so I was able to see somewhat. I knew it was dangerous, but I knew I really didn't have any other choice at that moment, either. I didn't even know if the fire department was coming. I didn't have a phone in my room to call, our only phone was in the kitchen, and if the neighbors hadn't seen or heard our fire alarm, then help wasn't coming.

With that startling realization, I forced my body to move once again, but only this time, I went out into the fire. I moved quickly, everything was hot, so very hot, and I knew if I hesitated or went too slowly it would swallow me whole. I had to move as swiftly as I could.

I could feel the heat on the bottoms of

my bare feet and I knew they would be burned within moments. I ran down the stairs, doing my best to jump over large spots of fire. When I reached the second floor, I couldn't believe how bad it was down there. I hadn't met my parents in the hallway or on the stairs and I was afraid that meant they were still in their room. The fire and smoke would have spread to their floor before mine, so there was a very real possibility that they were unconscious from the smoke.

I had to try to get to them.

I had to try and get them out.

I raced down the hallway as best as I could. My foot landed on the ground and a second later it was gone. I collapsed down hard with my foot hanging through the floor.

The fire was getting closer to me now.

HAWKE

A choked scream tried to escape my throat as my left forearm caught on fire. I pushed myself up and tried to get the fire out, but no matter what I did, I couldn't seem to get it out. I knew I needed to drop and roll, but there was fire all around me. If I did what I was supposed to do, what I had always been taught, the rest of me would catch on fire as well. I used my right hand and tried to pat the fire out as I moved to my parents' bedroom. Only, I quickly realized all of it was pointless, because the door had been completely burned away and their room was engulfed in flames. There was nothing left. If they had been in there, they were dead. No doubt about it.

I couldn't allow myself to think of that as the only possible outcome. I had to believe it was feasible that they couldn't get up to me, so they ran outside and called for help.

I promptly turned around and fled back down the hallway. I made sure to jump over the hole in the floor, and once I reached the next level of stairs, I literally flew down them. They were completely covered in fire and I could feel how weak the wood was underneath my burning feet. I could feel the wood giving away as my foot left the last step. I had to get out of there now or I would be trapped inside the house and burned alive.

Reaching the main level of my house, I didn't even take the time to look around. All I could see was the front door, or at least where the front door was supposed to be. It was no longer there and flames surrounded the frame. I didn't care, though, because just on the other side of those flames was my salvation. I would be outside and alive. I would be free from the smoke and the fire. Able to breathe again.

My arm was still smoldering and the pain of the scorched skin and muscle threatened to bring me to my knees, but I knew if that happened, if I went down and gave even another moment's thought to the excruciating pain in my arm and my charred feet, I would never make it out.

I refused to die when I was so close.

Blocking out the pain and the scorching heat surrounding me, I bolted the short distance from the bottom of the stairs and straight through the circle of flames.

The second I was outside, my body gave in and I collapsed onto the cool cement of the walkway at the front of my house. The last thing I saw before everything went black was my neighbor running toward me, and then I felt someone putting a coat over my arm to extinguish the flames.

***

Present Day...

I snapped up in my bed with a sharp indrawn breath, choking as a silent scream caught in my throat. That wasn't the first time I had been woken up by that nightmare. Hell, it wasn't even the thousandth time. One would think that after twenty-one years I wouldn't still be having the same nightmare. I should have been over it, but I guess there was no getting over a trauma like the one I had experienced.

Sometimes, I can still smell their burning flesh. It will strike me out of nowhere and I have to fight back the nausea that hits me like a ton of bricks. I was very tired of having the nightmares, fed up with reliving that night again and again, but I doubted it would ever end. After twenty-one years of having them almost nightly, and they were still going strong, I knew that meant they were not going to stop on their own. I suspected that the nightmares wouldn't end until I got closure, and I knew the only way I was going to get closure would be to find the arsonist who killed my parents and almost killed me.

One wouldn't think it would be possible for an arsonist to go unfound for twenty-one years. There should have been additional fires set after the one that killed my parents. There should have been evidence at other fires that this arsonist was out there, evidence that pointed to who he was and yet, I didn't even know his name. I didn't even know what he looked like.

My obsession with finding my parents' killer had led me to my career of being a fire investigator. I had gone through the Fire and Rescue Academy with the sole focus on becoming a fire investigator.

I took extra classes to ensure that I would be able to work in the investigation department and not be an active fire fighter. I had no problem with investigation work, but I did have a fear of fire. There was no way I would ever be able to run into a burning building every day for the rest of my life. I hadn't even known I was scared of fire until I had to run drills at the academy. I almost didn't make it, but I wasn't going to let my fear stop me from achieving my dreams. I'd pushed the fear down, I'd pushed the panic down, and I'd completed the drills and got through it. Thankfully, without anyone noticing that something was wrong with me. I hadn't risked losing my chance of finally achieving my goal.

I glanced over at the clock sitting on my bedside table and saw that it was four in the morning. The odds of me being able to get back to sleep were slim. I could never get my mind to shut off after a nightmare. Tossing the covers off,

I made my way over to my ensuite bathroom. I needed a shower to get the cold sweat off of me. It was a routine that I had long since grown accustomed to. I would wake up, take a shower, then start working. Sometimes if I felt like I needed the escape, I would go for a run. It wasn't often I went for a run, though. I wasn't a natural born runner. I really didn't like it, but every now and then it was the only way I could seem to get my mind to turn off for a little while. So whenever I was in need of a break from the darkness that threatened to consume me or when I needed my mind to see a puzzle from a different angle, I'd go for a run and it helped.

The hot water felt good against my cold skin. I always loved hot showers; there was something therapeutic about it. As if I could wash away the day or the nightmare away and when I came out, it was a fresh start. All of the bad or the trauma was gone and I was a completely different person.

I knew it was just shiny window dressing, I wasn't actually a different person, I was the same person with all of the same problems, but I told my mind I was different with the new vanity update.

I did it all just so I could keep going, go on making it through each day. Some days were harder than others. I wasn't depressed, I wouldn't go that far with it, but some days were certainly harder than others. I knew they would be when I decided to be a fire investigator.

I'd thought they would be hard because it would remind me of what happened growing up. I didn't even think that days could be hard because I had to witness the pain and destruction from each and every fire. Even the fires where no one was hurt or killed bothered me. To know that those people would have to rebuild, that they lost everything, it was devastating. I just needed to figure out how to handle it.

I'd fight through it one way or another.

Once the water turned cold, I climbed out. After quickly getting dried off, I got dressed in some sweats before I made my way out into the living room.

My apartment wasn't very big. I didn't have a need for a large house or condo. I didn't throw parties and I didn't have people over. Hell, I didn't even celebrate holidays.

HAWKE

Holidays used to be huge for my family growing up. I couldn't remember a single Christmas before the age of twelve where there weren't fifty people over for dinner. Our tree used to be nine feet tall with a hundred presents under it for all of the kids and family members. Christmas was always a big deal, same as Thanksgiving. Even Halloween, my parents would take a ton of photos and all of my cousins would come over and we would all go out trick or treating. It was always a big deal, no matter how small the holidays were.

Everything had changed after that night. I knew things would be different with their death, but I'd never expected for it to change so drastically.

My mother, she didn't have much in the way of family. She was an only child, didn't have any cousins, aunts, uncles, or even grandparents. It was just her and her parents. From what I knew from growing up with them and what my mother had mentioned, they weren't very loving people. They weren't bad people, they just weren't affectionate people.

After the fire, I'd lost my parents, I'd lost my home, I'd lost everything that I had for memories of them. All of that was to be expected, but what I hadn't expected, was losing my family.

My father had a big family with lots of cousins, siblings, aunts, and uncles. My grandparents on my father's side were both alive, too. Every weekend someone was at the house, but that all stopped when he died. With his death, it was like I suddenly didn't exist anymore. I didn't know if they felt like it was my fault somehow or if seeing me only reminded them of who they'd lost. Either way, they disappeared twenty-one years ago. I went from having a huge family with lots of birthday parties and holidays to sitting all alone at the dinner table every night.

I can still clearly remember the look on my maternal grandparents' faces when I told them that I wanted to be a fire investigator. It was the first time in the six years I had lived with them that they showed any emotion. Fear. It was the first and only time they had stated an opinion, that they tried to tell me what to do. They were furious at me for even thinking about being around a fire. They didn't understand that being a fire investigator didn't mean I would be running into burning buildings. I would be the one that investigated when a fire took place to ensure there was no foul play. It was different. But even after explaining it a hundred times, they didn't get it or they didn't care to. When I left at eighteen for the Fire and Rescue Academy, that was the last time I had seen or heard from them. It wasn't my doing, I had reached out plenty of times, but they refused to take my calls. They even moved so I couldn't stop by unannounced. Now, I look at the death notices in the paper every day to make sure they are both still alive.

I had some friends, but I kept them at a distance. I didn't really know why. It wasn't like I didn't know how to have friends. I had plenty growing up and even after my parents died I had some. Not as many as I used to, but more than

I could ever need.

I didn't know what happened, but as I got older, I started to lose friends and it was my own doing. I stopped reaching out to them, stopped calling or texting them back. I stopped going out with them. I stopped going out, period. I started to spend all of my time inside and researching.

My apartment was direct proof of my antisocial behavior. I had multiple white boards and bulletin boards that wheeled around. They were all filled with different fires that I suspected were arson, but I didn't have solid proof to bring anything to my Captain's attention yet. I was tracking their signatures and keeping an eye out for any reports of similar fires. When one came up, I would add it to my collection and after three with the same signature, I would finally have enough to bring it to my Captain's attention. I'd done that over two dozen times in the last decade. My work was my life and I wouldn't have it any other way.

I made my way over to the board that I had specifically for my parents' case. Their arsonist was still out there and despite the fact that I knew the chances of him still being active were slim, I was determined to find him. I knew people would probably call it an obsession, hell, it *was* an obsession, but I honestly couldn't think of anything more important to be obsessed over.

Subconsciously, I ran my fingers over the raised flesh of my left forearm where my scars were. It was a habit that I was aware of and yet, I couldn't seem to stop. It happened whenever I thought about my parents or a bad case.

My whole forearm was covered in ugly, multi-colored scars. I had received a third degree burn to it that night. When I had been in the hospital recovering from it, I didn't feel any pain at first, which was the only benefit from having a burn so severe. My feet, amazingly, hadn't been anywhere near as bad as I would've thought they'd be from walking over the fiery stairs and hallways. I'd received first degree burns on the bottoms of my feet and up my ankle on the left side. So yes, I had blisters and pain but nothing like I went through for my arm. That in and of itself was a miracle, I supposed, but one I was grateful for.

The recovery process on my arm was very painful once the burn started to heal. Having to have my burned skin scraped off over and over again as new skin started to regrow was excruciating. The risk of infection was so high, I had to spend two months in the hospital unable to leave or to see people. By the time I got out, I didn't really have anyone to see. My grandparents had even stopped coming by the hospital.

At first they never left.

They would stand outside of my room looking through the glass wall for hours just so they could keep me company. It didn't matter that we couldn't talk, they were there for me. At least for the first two weeks before every day all day turned into every other day for a few hours, until it finally, slowly, dwindled down to nothing at all. At that point, the only people I saw were the doctors or nurses that came into my room to check my arm over and the people walking by.

I used to spend hours trying to figure out who the people were, what their story was. I would look out that glass wall and watch the people buzzing around as if it was my own live theatre. As weird as it was, it kept me sane for those very long two months I spent in the hospital.

Letting out a long sigh, I ran a hand through my hair and shook my head to try to dispel the memories that had crept up on me once more. I made my way into my kitchen. I needed coffee and then I would get back to work. I was going to crack my parents' case, no matter how long it took me.

CHAPTER TWO

Hawke

AT THE SOUND of my alarm going off, I reached over and turned it off without even opening my eyes. I was not ready to be awake yet. I used to love waking up; it was one of the best parts of my day. I used to wake up and roll over to wrap my arms around Paul.

We didn't live together, but we spent

every single night over at my place. Paul and I had been dating for two years and it got pretty serious awfully quick. Within two months, he was practically living with me. I had never seen his place, not even to this day. I had no idea what it looked like or where it even was. He was always over at mine. At first, I'd just figured he was a messy person and he knew I was a more clean and organized person so my place is where I'd be more comfortable.

In hindsight, that was my first red flag.

I didn't have a set type, I was more interested in the man's personality, if he was a good person and had strong morals. That was what mattered most to me over body shape or hair color.

Paul was a cop, a good cop. He loved

to help people and children. He seemed like a great guy and I quickly fell for him and I thought he'd fallen for me just as fast. We spent so much time together, especially in my apartment.

We used to try and go out on dates, but we could never keep our hands off of each other. In the beginning, I thought it was great that we were so attracted to each other that we couldn't go a single minute without touching the other. Not to mention the sex was off-the-wall amazing. As time went on, though, I quickly discovered that the reason he never took me out on dates was because he was very deep in the closet. That him using sex to make us miss our movie or reservation was just his way of keeping me as his dirty secret. He was using sex to get what he wanted and I had fallen for it. Hook. Line. And sinker.

I wasn't too happy about him being in the closet, but I had tried hard to understand it. To deal with it for the sake of our relationship. I was a firefighter and I understood that the people we worked with were not always open-minded. First responders could be homophobic, more so than people realized. They had no problem saving gay people and protecting them, but they didn't want to work next to one. To most of them, if a man was gay then they would most likely be gawking at them in the shower or when they were changing. They automatically assumed that every gay man wanted every man. They failed to realize that it was the same as it was for straight men. Straight men didn't find every female attractive, and we didn't find every male attractive. Getting someone who was homophobic to understand that though, was like trying to convince a brick wall it was really a door.

My issue wasn't so much that Paul was in the closet. My issue was that he didn't even want to be seen outside of work around me, because I was out and proud. He thought and felt that if people in his precinct saw us together they would assume he was gay as well.

We were *never* allowed to be seen together out in public.

There were no dates, just dinner and a movie inside my apartment. The blinds were always closed, just in case someone drove by or walked by and just happened to see us together. When we did have to interact at work, which was thankfully, very rarely, he basically ignored me. He would talk to anyone else, going out of his way to ignore me like all the other officers. His image was more important to him than being a decent human being, and for two years I put up with it because he promised me he would come out. He promised me that things would change and we could be together like a normal couple. That he was going to show everyone in his precinct that him being gay didn't change who he was.

It all sounded amazing. It *sounded* perfect. Paul was a man's man. He loved playing sports, he liked to go hunting with the guys, he worked on cars, and he was a gym addict. He was very much the very definition of a *manly* man. He was the perfect example to show people that being gay didn't make you feminine or a fairy. That men could be gay and still love cars and sports. He would have started the long overdue process for the homophobes in the police force to start to see gay men as something more than the stereotype they placed them in. It would have been our chance to have a true relationship like everyone else.

Only after two years, Paul didn't come out.

I lived for two years of Paul and his excuses as to why he couldn't come out yet. At first, he said he was new to the precinct and he wanted to make friends first so they would know him before he came out. Then, it was he got a new Commanding Officer who was homophobic and he had to wait until the guy was transferred. Then, it became he wanted to get his detective shield first so he couldn't have his sexuality used against him. It was just one excuse after the next, and I had quickly started to reach the end of my rope with him.

All of that changed, though, when I went into a local bar for first responders and saw that everyone was celebrating. Paul was there with his new fiancée, Stacey. They had been dating for four years, living together for two. It was a slap in the face to discover that I was the dirty mistress. That the reason I had never been to his place was because he had his girlfriend living there.

I'd felt so sick to my stomach. I'd wanted to yell out right there in that bar that Paul had just fucked me the night before. To whip out my phone and show them the photos of us together. Make him admit that we had been in a relationship, and not just to force him out of the closet, but because Stacey deserved to know. Whether Paul was bisexual or not, she deserved to know that her boyfriend, now fiancé, had been cheating on her for two years. That he liked to sleep with men.

What made it come out of left field for me, though, was the fact that he'd always bottomed with me. I was a top, I wasn't a bottom, and I wasn't a switch, I only ever topped. I never expected for Paul to ever be a top with a man or a woman.

He absolutely *loved* being a bottom.

He loved being dominated.

He loved it rough.

To me, I'd never cared for rough sex. I loved passionate sex, but to me that was rough sex. Paul loved it when there were bruises left behind from me holding his wrists or grabbing his hips tightly. I never cared for it, but I wanted to give him the best sex he could have, so I played along. That is something that I definitely wouldn't miss about being with Paul. I wouldn't miss the rough sex and having to always be in control in the bedroom. I loved doing different positions and not just the same ones. I loved laying back and watching my man ride me, but that was something that Paul never wanted.

I was sure that a Shrink would say that Paul needed it to hurt, that he needed to feel like he was being dominated so he could feel good. That he wasn't ready to accept that he was gay, so the roughness allowed his mind to be fooled into what was happening. Or perhaps that he didn't have a choice in the act so it was okay to enjoy it.

It was messed up and I was relieved that I wouldn't have to be a part of that any longer.

After the hurt and anger had disappeared, I started to feel sorry for Paul and for Stacey. I felt sorry for her because the man she was in love with, the man she was set to marry, was living a lie. She was going to marry a man who she truly didn't know. That wasn't fair to her. I knew most people would be mad and angry at her, but it wasn't her fault. I was sure she would blame me if she knew I existed, but it wasn't my fault either. We both didn't know about the other. That was on Paul. Paul was the only one to blame for his betrayal and it was really sad for Stacey because she might have to get divorced. I just hoped they didn't get pregnant. No child deserves to come into a home like the one Paul was creating. A home built on lies and deceit.

I felt sorry for Paul, too. Everyone at the firehouse thought I should still be pissed off at him and trying to cut his balls off. And I had been, at first, but now I thought it was just sad. He was sad and a bit pathetic. He was so afraid to accept who he was that he was willing to be miserable and live a lie for who knew how many more years. He could have been happy. All he had to do was accept that he was gay.

It was the twenty-first century, for fuck's sake.

It wasn't like he was going to be

stoned to death in the middle of the street. Yes, he was going to have to deal with assholes inside the force, and some in public, too, there were homophobic asshats everywhere still, but he would find friends like I had who would stand up for him and stand by him. He would at least have a chance at having a real life with a loving and healthy relationship. He was throwing everything away because of his fear and that was no way to live.

I let out a groan as I rubbed a hand over my face and tried to wake up. I had to get to work soon so I needed to get up and start getting ready. I was on day shifts this week and I was thankful for the break from the night shifts. I didn't mind the night shifts, but it made for a long day. I also preferred to not be sleeping all day long and to get to be out in the sunlight. It was also easier to get things done around the house when I was getting home at a decent hour.

Letting out one more groan, I pushed myself up and climbed out of bed. I grabbed a change of clothes and took a quick shower. After grabbing some breakfast, I made my way out of my apartment and took off for the firehouse.

After parking my car on the street, I made the short walk to the firehouse. I was a late bloomer, as the guys like to call me. I was thirty, but I had only worked as a firefighter for five years now. I hadn't joined the academy until I was twenty-five and most people who joined did so between eighteen and twenty.

I hadn't known what I wanted to do for a living. I hadn't known what my calling was. Instead of going to college and putting myself into debt, I'd decided to do different jobs. I'd worked minimum wage jobs and volunteered at other jobs to see what I enjoyed the most. I'd wanted to do something that I loved and I'd wanted to know what that would be before I started my career. I didn't want to be one of these people who went to college and didn't know what they wanted to do so they racked up student debt only to graduate and still not enjoy their career. I'd wanted to be sure that I loved the career that I'd chosen. So I volunteered at various different businesses. I volunteered at a veterinary clinic, a lawyer's office, a restaurant, a day care, a doctor's office, and even a physiotherapist's office. I'd tried all of those different potential careers, but none of them stuck with me. I hadn't felt like they were meant for me. Like they were the type of career I could spend my life in and be happy.

All of that changed one night when I'd been driving down the road and saw a car accident happen right in front of me. Witnessing the carnage shook me to my core.

My reaction even more so.

I had instantly pulled over and jumped out of my car to go over to help the victims from the cars. The crash had very bad and the one car had flipped upside down. I hadn't been able get the woman out, but I'd stayed there on the ground with her, talking to her and trying to help her remain calm and awake until the firefighters arrived.

Standing back and watching them all

work, I'd felt mesmerized. They'd all worked together with the ambulance attendants to help secure the woman on a backboard and get her out of the car and off to the hospital. The way they'd interacted with each other and the victims, it felt like a family to me and that was something I'd realized I wanted more than anything. That same day, I had called and asked if I could volunteer at a firehouse to see what it was like to be a firefighter.

I'd gone to volunteer at a firehouse two weeks later and I fell in love.

It was the brotherhood that I wanted. The brotherhood of them all being there for each other, the way they were a family.

I grew up in the foster system. I had no idea who my biological parents were, if they were even alive. I had been passed around from one home to the next my whole life. When I was fourteen, I had been placed in a group home for teenage boys that was more like a jail than a home. I had been abused, neglected, and pretty much left to fend for myself basically my whole life. So to me there was a huge appeal to being a member of a family.

To be a brother in a *real* family.

The idea of running into a burning building never bothered me. It had never even crossed my mind that I would have to be surrounded by fire or put into a dangerous position to help save someone. To me, it was all worth it if I could be a member of a family. Finally, I'd found my calling. A career where my gut told me I would be happy to go to work each day.

I'd signed up for the academy that very same day and I flew through it. The physical aspect of it was very easy for me and I had no problem with the classroom work. I had always been good at school, even if I didn't show up often because of the foster parents. I took everything I could from the academy, aware that any of it could be what helped me to keep my new brothers safe. I took it seriously and I made sure I would be ready for anything that would come my way once I became a firefighter. Once I graduated, I had been placed as a probie in Firehouse Twenty-One and I hadn't regretted a single moment.

"Hey man," Zander said, flashing me a warm smile as he wiped down the driver's side door of engine forty-three.

Zander was always washing the trucks. He loved to keep them shiny and he loved the busy work of it. Zander was a car guy and he loved working on them, even if that was just washing and polishing them. He had two big fire trucks to keep his hands busy and you could find him in the garage doing something with them more often than not.

"Hey, how was the overnight?"

"The guys said it was a pretty quiet night. They were able to sleep most of it away, lucky bastards."

"That's good, though, and hey, maybe it'll be quiet today," I said, flashing my own hopeful smile.

Before Zander could say anything, the alarm from our overheard speaker rang out, followed by the dispatcher's voice over the intercom as they requested our truck for a fire in progress. The second the dispatcher's voice disappeared, Zander gave me a look and I knew what he was thinking.

"You just had to say the Q-word."

"Yup, that was my bad," I agreed, before we ran off to get our gear on.

I really shouldn't have said anything. I knew better than to say the word *quiet* while on shift. All of us knew better because usually, that is when shit hit the fan. This time around it was completely my bad and hopefully, Zander didn't rat me out to the guys. The last thing I wanted to do today was scrub the bathrooms for using the q-word.

We all loaded up and headed off for the fire. I was hoping it wouldn't be too bad, that we could get there before the fire ate up the whole house. It was a toss up on whether we would be able to save the house or not. We always hoped that we could. We didn't want to leave anyone without a home. We knew how devastating that could be and we never wanted to cause someone that pain. Unfortunately, we didn't always have a say in what happened. It really depended on the fire and how hot it was burning.

The second we pulled up to the house, we all could see that the flames were out of control. Local police were already on the scene and trying to escort everyone away from the house. I knew they would have already been evacuating the nearby homes in case the flames jumped to the other houses, too. We jumped out and instantly got to work on getting the hoses out.

"Hawke, Zander, get hose one set up. Jase and Gage, get hose two set up and get it around the back. We need to hit this from both sides," Captain Clark called out.

Zander and I quickly ran and got our hose started. The fire was burning hot and fast and I couldn't help but wonder if an accelerant had been used. The trick was, house fires could go up quickly with the furniture in the home. It could also burn faster depending on when the house was built. Different building materials could make the house burn faster. Once we got the fire under control, we would be able to go through it and see what the cause was.

With our hose hooked up to the fire hydrant, Zander and I went over to the front door that was engulfed in flames and turned the water on. I was ready for the power of the water that shot out of the nozzle. I was in front and controlling the hose and where the water was sprayed. The power of the water being pushed out had surprised me at first when I was in the academy and now it was a comfort. I knew that as long as that power was there, then the water was coming and we would be able to gain control of the fire.

As the flames started to dissipate, we made our way into the house. I could see Jase and Gage on the other side of the house working their way toward us. The stairs were gone and the top floor of the house had crashed down to the main level. If we had taken any longer to get here, there wouldn't have been anything left. Working together, we were able to get the flames out until all that was left of the house was a wet, charred mess. Zander took our hose back to the truck as Gage and I started to look through the rubble to see if there had been anyone inside. The police didn't know because the neighbors didn't know. The woman who owned the house didn't have a car, so we couldn't look to see if there was a car there. I was hoping and praying that the woman who lived there was not in there. That she had been at work or out shopping when the first started.

"Cap, we got a body," Gage's voice came over our radio.

"Shit," I said to myself.

I hated this part of the job. This was the part of the job that no one could prepare you for. No one could prepare you for finding someone who had been trapped and unable to escape from a fire. There were a lot of ways to die, but to me getting burned alive had to be the worst. Whenever we came across a body in a fire, I always hoped that they had died from smoke inhalation long before the flames got to them. It wasn't ideal, but at least the smoke would make them pass out so they wouldn't have felt any pain as they died. Most of the time, that was the case and I was forever thankful that they could go in a somewhat peaceful manner.

"Copy. I'll call the Investigation Unit. Keep searching for anyone else just in case she had a visitor over," Captain Clark said through the radio.

"Copy," I said back as I silently sent

up a prayer that the body would be the only one we recovered today.

CHAPTER THREE

Tristan

PULLING UP TO the crime scene, I already had a bad feeling in the pit of my stomach. Every crime scene brought that same feeling to my belly. I was always waiting for the day that I would come across the same arsonist who had killed my parents.

He was still out there.

I knew in my gut he was.

I couldn't explain it, but I could just *feel* it. He was out there, mocking me with each fire he set.

I had dedicated my life to finding and stopping arsonists, to preventing people from going through the horrific trauma that I had experienced. And yet, I couldn't seem to find one man, the man who gave me my scars and nightmares.

I knew rationally and logically that he was most likely dead. It had been twenty-one years. He wouldn't have been young based on the skill that he used on my home back then. Arsonists tended to either get caught or kill themselves in one of their fires. They didn't tend to be able to dodge the police for very long.

Most people would assume that catching an arsonist was difficult with the fire destroying all of the evidence, and what the fire didn't destroy, the firefighters certainly did. Not that it was their fault, of course. The water was necessary to prevent further damage. The only way to put out a fire was with water, but unfortunately, water tended to destroy any evidence that the fire didn't eat away in its path. Still, a trained eye could read a burned down building and determine how the fire was started and find evidence that pointed to the arsonist.

The psychological profile of an arsonist also did them no favors. Arsonists, even at a young age, they tended to stand out. People remembered them. More often than not, when I had a suspect and spoke with neighbors, family, and friends, they always said the same kind of thing, 'He's always been a bit weird.' It didn't come as a shock or a surprise to people, not like it did with some of the best serial killers. Arsonists didn't tend to blend in and hide well in society, and nine out of ten times, they had their own burns from their earlier days of experimenting.

What frustrated me the most, though, was knowing that I couldn't catch my parents' killer and yet, so far I caught any other arsonist who came into my path. It was frustrating and I would be lying if I said it wasn't affecting my self-confidence.

How was it I couldn't catch one arsonist?

He was just a man and he was out there, and yet I couldn't even put a face to the man.

My newest crime scene was abuzz with life. Onlookers stood on the other side of the yellow police tape. Most of them looked worried and horrified at the destruction of someone's home. Others had a look that told me they were trying to figure out how to leave without coming across as insensitive. It was human nature to want to gawk at something horrible, just as it was human nature to want to get on with life and be thankful it wasn't you.

I ignored those natural human reactions and scanned the crowd to see if I could find one that wasn't natural in the face of destruction such as this. Arsonists loved to see their handy work. They loved to watch the fire grow and consume. All too often they hid away in the crowd to see the end result. Fire starting was a compulsion, an addiction, and not something that could be stopped on their own. Much like a drug addict or an alcoholic, they couldn't stop setting fires without getting treatment. Unfortunately though, unlike a normal drug addiction, arsonists weren't just inflicting pain onto themselves. Their addiction destroyed lives by either destroying a home or killing someone.

Having your house destroyed might not seem like that big of a deal to some. Not when compared to your life being taken or that of someone you loved. However, it was equally devastating to know that every single thing you owned was lost. Yes, it was just stuff, material possessions, but sometimes that stuff had sentimental meaning. Photos of loved ones who had passed, a child's favorite stuffed animal or blanket that they needed in order to fall asleep at night, a dead parent's shirt with their scent that still lingered on it. Those items couldn't be replaced and there was no monetary amount that would ever be enough compensation for them.

Even the annoyance of having to live somewhere else until they were able to rebuild or find a new home could be too much for some people. Most people couldn't afford to start all over again and often they ended up in a shelter with nothing but whatever clothes had been donated to them. There was more than one way for a person to lose their life in a fire and unfortunately, unless a person were lucky enough to have it contained quickly, they were going to lose their life one way or the other long before the fire got put out.

With the fire out the firefighters were working on cleaning up now. Some were getting their tools and the fire hoses back onto the truck and in the proper order. Others, the more experienced firefighters for the station house, were inside the burned out shell of the house and going through it to try and figure out how the fire got started.

Not every fire required an investigator to be on scene for it. Often seasoned firefighters could find the origin of the fire and determine what ignited it without assistance from an investigator. Most of the time it was a candle that had been left too close to a curtain, or someone dropped a lit cigarette into the couch and thought there was no burning ash left behind, or a kitchen fire when someone wasn't being as careful as they should be with things on the stove. Oil fires were the biggest issues when it came to a kitchen blaze. People just didn't take care and didn't realize how quickly things could go wrong when it came to oil and fire, and then of course, many exacerbated the issue by panicking and making the mistake of putting water on an oil fire, and well, that just made everything so much worse. Oil and water didn't mix. Add in a heat source igniting that oil and it just accelerated the fire, made it spread even more when water was added.

Most fires were accidental or they were electrical. Calling an investigator in meant that something more was going on this time around. The sight of the coroner's van only cemented that probability. A dead victim meant that the fire had been placed in one of two categories.

The first category meant it was an accidental fire or a non-human started fire, meaning it was a structural issue such as faulty electrical, and the occupant was not able to get out. They could have been trapped in a room or they could have died from smoke inhalation before they even made it out of their bed.

The other category was arson. That meant someone purposely started the fire and made sure the occupant could not escape.

It was my job to determine which one it was.

For me, most of the time it was either an accident or some type of structural issue. Out of date electrical, a water heater that was too old and exploded, insulation that caught fire from being around a heating source that went against building codes. Seven out of ten times it was not an arsonist, but someone still had to be held accountable for it.

I had helped to arrest over three hundred contractors and developers for their part in a deadly fire. All of which typically had the same excuse every single time: corners needed to be cut because they were on a tight budget and so they hired handymen instead of licensed professionals. Shady contractors cost the world more damage than most people even realized.

I made my way into the mostly burned down house to see Captain

William Clark as well as one of his firefighters. The back of his coat said Colton. I had dealt with a lot of different fire houses in the city and it wasn't the first time I'd worked with Station House Twenty-One, but I hadn't worked with Colton before. I hadn't heard anything about him, but it was possible he was newer.

Captain Clark was known to be a tough captain. He was very professional and he was known to be distant. From what I had seen and based on what I had heard through the grapevine, he kept his men at arm's length, but I couldn't hold that against him.

I myself didn't have close friends, or any friends at all. I didn't let the people that I worked with get to know me. I preferred to keep that level of professionalism between us. I didn't want to get involved in their personal lives and I held no interest in having them poking their noses into mine.

Interestingly enough though, Captain Clark had allegedly been recently warming up to his men. I suspected it had to do with his new boyfriend, Noah Riley. He used to be a Federal Prosecutor but from what I had heard he was now a law professor at the University and he helped the Federal Protection Agency with special cases. Up until recently, Captain Clark had been in the closet and when he announced his relationship to Noah everyone at the office began talking about it.

I never contributed to the conversation. Mostly because I wasn't looking to get into a debate about having homosexuals in a First Responders position. Even though it was the twenty-first century, there were still homophobes everywhere. People often still had that stereotype of what a gay man looked and acted like, and it never tended to be a strong, muscular man who risked his life to save people.

I knew that it would be hard for the Captain. Even though he was a Captain, it wouldn't change the fact that people in the fire department would have an issue with him being gay. It would be even harder for those who came out as gay and were ranked lower. Unfortunately, an all men's club was not very welcoming to those who preferred the company of men to women.

"Captain," I said as I walked over to Captain Clark.

HAWKE

"Investigator Cole, it's nice to see you again. Though I wish it was for different circumstances. This is one of my newer guys, Hawke Colton. Hawke, this is Tristan Cole, one of the best fire investigators I've had the pleasure of working with."

Colton, or Hawke, turned around and I was instantly taken back by how attractive he was. He wasn't wearing a helmet so I could see that he had medium length, light brown hair. It had a slight wave to it and my fingers itched to run through it. His eyes were sky blue and he had high cheekbones. Honestly, he looked like he'd just walked off the cover of a firefighter calendar. As if Mr. June was standing right there in front of me. He gave me a warm smile that almost made my knees go weak.

"It's nice to meet you, Inspector Cole," Hawke said as he held his hand out for me to shake.

"It's nice to meet you." I clasped his hand in mine as I spoke. He was wearing his thick firefighter gloves, but even still when our hands touched I felt a wave of heat starting to spread up my arm from my hand. I had felt something like that before, but it was only skin on skin and it was never anything that intense.

Maybe I did need to get laid.

"What do we have?" I asked, trying to move on and forget about the warmth that was still lingering in my body even after he'd pulled his hand away.

"We have one body, a female, most likely the owner of the house. Local PD are asking around and trying to see if our victim was the only occupant in the house. At first glance, it appears that a candle was left on," Captain Clark started.

"Okay, but I'm here so I'm guessing that you decided the initial glance wasn't correct," I said as I took in the room.

Everything was black. The whole place had gone up and I knew that a house could effortlessly burn down without an accelerant being used. We'd come a long way in making safe products for our homes, but fabric was still flammable. Rugs could burn quickly, curtains, furniture. Almost everything in a home could work as its own accelerant without too much difficulty. All it needed was a flame to get them going. It made it very easy for inexperienced fire investigators to suspect arson when it was just a terrible accident. At the same time though, it was easy for an arsonist to use the items in their victim's home to make it burn hotter and faster. They could use what was already in the house to cover their tracks and get away with arson.

It was also a defense attorney's wet dream.

They loved to argue that we got it wrong, that it was all an accident. It made our job harder, because we had to find additional evidence to make the case stick. Sometimes there wasn't additional evidence, because it was destroyed in the fire. Too many times arsonists got to walk and there was nothing we could do but keep going and hope the next time we could get them.

"Potentially. After the initial search, we started to look at the wiring and electrical boxes to see if they were the source of the fire. There are no obvious accelerants or origin of the fire, the electrical box, though, is telling a different story," Captain Clark said as he walked toward what was left of the back of the house.

"As you can see, the burn pattern is coming from the main electrical box. When we opened it, we expected to find frayed wires, clear evidence that it was overloaded. Only, we found this." Captain Clark held out a small metal rectangular device. It was all melted together, but I could see the different wire circuit built onto the device.

I had seen this before, and it was a signature that I knew all too well. The device worked as an incendiary device. The arsonist would place it within the electrical box and turn it on. It would slowly start to heat up and once it got hot enough, it caused the wires in the electrical box to start to melt and an electrical fire would be set in motion. Most of the time if it was discovered investigators or firefighters just assumed it was part of the electrical box and ignored it.

I knew better, though.

I had seen it before in the fire that took my parents' lives.

The arsonist had used that exact type of device.

"Have you found any type of camera in your search?" I asked.

The arsonist who killed my parents had been able to see his artwork with hidden cameras that he had placed all throughout the house. Finding those cameras had ultimately been the deciding factor on if my parents' fire was accidental or not.

The fire investigator had discarded the incendiary device that they found in the electrical box, the same device that I was currently holding. When he found the cameras, though, he knew something else was going on. They were hidden in places that people wouldn't put a surveillance camera.

The investigator had grilled me in the hospital about everyone who had been in my house or had access to it. Nothing ever came from it and now the device and everything else sat in a box marked *cold case*, but I was determined to make sure it was marked *closed* one day.

"Not yet, we haven't done a full sweep. Do you suspect we'll find any?"

Captain Clark asked, and I could hear the interest in his voice.

"If it's who I think it is, yes. You'll find them hidden within the walls in protective cases. They'll have burnt up in the fire, but you'll find melted plastic where it shouldn't be."

"We'll look through the debris and see what we can find. It's going to take the better part of the day. You won't have my report until tomorrow, at the earliest."

I nodded in acknowledgement of his words. I knew it would take some time for them to comb through everything. Fire was always a mess and firefighters, unfortunately, made it worse. I would be lucky if I was able to get the report tomorrow, it all depended on what they could find. I had what I needed for today, though. I had the device. Now I just needed to convince my boss that this was connected to my parents' fire.

***

Walking into my boss' office, I had already prepared myself for a war. This wasn't the first time I'd come to speak with my boss about a fire that I believed, that I *knew* in my gut, was connected to my parents' fire.

The cameras connected the crime scenes. They were a very specific brand of camera that had been discontinued fifteen years ago. I had been trying to track down wholesale or bulk purchases, but so far I was striking out. There had been over a hundred suppliers for the cameras and they subcontracted their products to other smaller shops. It was a mess and a very long list, but I wasn't going to give up.

The cameras connected my parents' killer to thirty-five other fires that I'd discovered so far. I didn't work every case and not all investigators liked to share. There were also fires that were investigated but deemed accidental. I suspected there were more, most likely they had been closed as accidental because the investigator missed something. I'd like to say that every investigator was a good one, but it was just like every other job. They had star employees, they had the employees that were middle of the road, and then they have the employees that were just there for the paycheck and didn't care.

"Tristan, what brings you in?"

My boss, Captain Damon Amaro, was

thirty-eight and had been on the job since he was eighteen. He was a good man, single and no kids. He worked a lot and he didn't care for the political aspect of the job. Not that I could blame him. I never enjoyed having to play nice with others, either. I was also very bad at it. It's why I would never make Captain. I didn't see the point in kissing someone's ass. If I was good at my job, then it shouldn't matter what social skills I had. My promotion shouldn't be connected to how many parties I went to or how many times I play golf with the boys. Not that I play golf. Hell, I couldn't hit a golf ball if my life depended on it.

"A fire at 1583 Bartlett Street is going to be marked as arson. This device was found in the electrical box," I started as I placed the evidence bag down on his desk.

"How many people know about these things," he asked as he examined the device.

"Captain Clark is looking now for any cameras. I suspect he will find at least ten like the other crime scenes." I stopped as he held his hand up and cut me off.

"You don't know that. We've had this conversation before, Tristan. Not every arsonist who uses this device is the same arsonist that killed your parents. I don't have to tell you the likelihood of this being the same arsonist."

"I understand that, Captain, but if the cameras are found and it comes back as the same cameras from the other thirty-five cases, that's a huge coincidence that you can't ignore," I countered.

"Even if I were to entertain this farfetched idea, you have to look at the facts, Tristan. Thirty-five cases with cameras that were sold by a lot of stores and suppliers. Not all of those fires had this device used, and there have been other fires that did use this device and there were no cameras. Even if I considered this theory the only way it could be the same arsonist is if he started in his early teens for the fire at your parents' house or he's well into his sixties now. You know the odds on that. We've discussed this. Every time cameras are found you try and see a connection to your parents' murder. I can't keep having this dialogue with you, Tristan. It's time you finally dealt with what happened to you growing up. Now, do I need to put you on administrative leave so you can get some help, or will you finally go and speak to a therapist?"

He was never going to believe me. I knew that, I did. No one was ever going to believe me because he was right. Arsonists typically didn't tend to live that long. If they didn't get arrested, their own fire killed them. And this arsonist was changing up his method all the time, but the one thing that stayed consistent was the cameras.

The guy had a huge body count and I knew he wasn't going to stop until we caught him. He was too smart to get eaten by his own fire. The only way to stop him would be to finally catch him. And the only way my boss or anyone was going to believe me was with irrefutable proof and it was on me to find it.

"No Sir, you don't need to put me on leave. Now if that is all, Sir, I have paperwork."

He didn't want to believe me. That was fine. I would prove it, because I was not going to allow the man responsible for my parents' death, for the death of fifty-eight people, to go unpunished. They all deserved justice and I would make sure they got it, even if it killed me.

CHAPTER FOUR

Hawke

IT HAD BEEN one of those days where all I wanted to do was go and get a stiff drink. Twelve-hour shifts were always hard, but it was worse when your shift started with a dead body.

There was this old superstition of sorts that every firehouse had. If your shift started off with a successful fire—

meaning the house was saved and no one died or was hurt—then your shift was going to be easy. If your shift started with a failed fire—meaning the house was destroyed or someone died—then your shift was going to be a nightmare and make you beg for the end of the day to arrive.

Today had only solidified the superstition in full force.

After the fire this morning, we had been going non-stop all day. There was a factory fire that burned so hot we lost the building completely and eighteen people had to be sent to the hospital for minor burns and smoke inhalation. Before we even made it back to the firehouse, we were sent on another call for a car crash that involved ten cars and a transport truck. The transport truck driver had hit a car that, according to witnesses, had cut the truck off and the truck driver couldn't stop in time. That driver we had to literally scrape off of the road. The truck driver was fine, but the truck went up in flames. The other cars were total losses and every person in the cars, all twenty of them, had to get some form of medical attention. And all of that was before lunchtime. After twelve hours, I was more than ready for a drink. Thankfully, I had a whole bottle of whiskey at home calling my name.

I headed out and made my way to my truck. Tomorrow was my day off and I was looking forward to the break. Twelve-hour shifts weren't easy. I had gotten used to them, for the most part, but sometimes it wasn't easy getting through the long shifts. Being a firefighter was just like any other job in that sense. Some days the hours flew by and others the time crawled by, it felt like you had been there for twelve days without an end in sight. Today had been one of those felt like forever days and I was looking forward to spending the day tomorrow just relaxing and recuperating after the trying day today.

What I had not expected was to see Investigator Cole standing next to my truck. He looked tired, drawn and disappointed maybe, but I could also see the determination in his eyes even from my short distance away. It was clear something must have happened and he must need some type of help from me. I couldn't help but wonder if it had to do with the body we found this morning.

HAWKE

I was still having a hard time with what I had seen. It wasn't the first time I had seen a dead body in a fire, of course. Hell, it wasn't even the thirtieth, but for some reason the image of her body was trapped in my mind. I knew it had only just happened roughly twelve hours ago and my mind still needed time to process it, but for some reason I felt like I would carry the woman's death with me for the rest of my life.

I was usually pretty good at moving on from a bad fire. Not holding on to any of the images or the people. Every firefighter was taught to not carry the victims with you, whether they survived or not. We didn't check up on patients, we didn't follow up with any of the investigations unless we were asked for assistance. That had happened before where we needed to take a fire investigator back to the crime scene and help walk them through it again. But we had always been taught to see the crime scenes as just evidence. The bodies are evidence, the destruction is evidence, and none of that needs to have an emotional attachment to it. More often than not, I could keep myself objective and distant from the crime scenes, from the deaths, and yet this time around I was having a harder time. I couldn't help but suspect that it had something to do with Investigator Tristan Cole.

The man was very attractive; anyone would have to be a fool to not see that. It was more than just his very attractive face and body. There was something in his eyes, a pain there. I could tell he was trying to hide it, trying to continue living his life as if he was like everyone else, but I could see it.

How could I miss it?

I saw that pain in my own eyes every time I looked at a mirror. It was the pain from a hard upbringing. The pain from not belonging anywhere, not feeling love like all of the other children did. It was not easy to live with and it often left me feeling like there was this giant hole in my chest. For the longest time I felt like I was never going to belong anywhere. That everyone could see the hole inside of me and they were all judging me for it. It took a long time before I was able to finally feel complete. Sure, there are days where I still feel like there is this huge piece of me missing, but for the most part, I finally felt whole. Being a firefighter and having brothers in my life had helped me greatly. Based on the look in Tristan's eyes, though, he didn't have anyone in his corner to help ease the pain he felt.

"Investigator Cole, what can I do for you," I asked once I was close enough.

"I'm sorry to drop by unannounced. I need some off-the-books help. All of the other investigators who I've spoken to have all said that you are one of the best firefighters they have worked with. They actually said they were surprised that you weren't an investigator yourself."

"I prefer the work on the front line."

I never thought I would ever be good at investigative work, but I had learned pretty quickly that I was observant and that helped in investigations. I was also good at reading people. Both of which was a direct result of growing up in foster care. If you weren't good at reading people and being observant, then you were at a great risk of being hurt. I had been hurt plenty of times before I learned that lesson.

It wasn't unusual for other fire investigators to speak with me about a case they were working. They would ask me to review their case file or walk through the crime scene to see if something was missed. I didn't mind doing it. When a crime had been committed or when a terrible accident occurred, everyone involved deserved to know the truth. If I could help them discover the truth, I was all for it. However, I did prefer to work in the firehouse alongside my brothers. I loved going into the fires and helping to stop them and save lives. That was who I was and I wasn't about to change that for a desk job, even one as important and rewarding as fire investigations.

"So I've heard. I have also heard that you are very good for someone who has been on the front lines as little of a time as you have been. People say you were born to be a firefighter. You have a knack for seeing patterns, for spotting things that other investigators have missed or overlooked. I'd hoped perhaps you would consider lending me that skill set with a case I am working on."

I'd suspected he was there for help on a case, but it still hurt to hear my suspicions confirmed. I would have been very interested if he'd wished to see me outside of work for a more personal matter. I didn't know if I was ready for a relationship after my latest disaster of one, but I was very much interested in getting back on the horse, so to speak.

I had a feeling Tristan had one hell of a horse to hop on.

Of course, this very sexy man just wanted me for my mind, typical story of my life, and there was a very good chance Tristan wasn't even gay. I didn't know much of anything about him. Nothing, really. I hadn't asked around about him or anything, but when I did work with other investigators none of them had ever mentioned anything about him, either. A good number of investigators had spoken about others, gossiped, really.

It was funny, in high school people told themselves that the gossiping would stop once they graduated, only to find that it didn't ever stop. It actually got worse as an adult. The problems that the other students were gossiping about in school were minute compared to the adult problems they had. Because of that, the gossip usually spread faster and it could be like trying to walk through a minefield without a map.

"I'm always happy to help out with an investigation. Is it the one from this morning?"

"It is. Amanda Rollins, thirty-five, single, no kids. She had a younger sibling but she died in a car accident five years ago. Her parents are both alive and are local. I have already spoken with them and they are hopeful for answers," Tristan started.

"Do you have any leads?"

Arson was one of the funny crimes, not that killing someone in a fire is funny, but it could be both personal and distant. An arsonist could target a home because they had a grudge against someone or the person represented someone else they had a grudge against, much like a serial killer killing only middle-aged redheads. However, arsonists could also target a home because it was convenient and easy to get to. They didn't always have an agenda of killing someone, often it was just an unfortunate side effect from the fire. An arsonist's only goal was to make a big fire and watch it eat everything in its path. Ms. Rollins' arsonist could be either option, and the first step to an arson investigation was to determine whether it was an opportunity or personal.

"Sort of, it's a bit complicated. My gut

is telling me that Ms. Rollins was another victim to a long-time arsonist that I have been trying to find for the past fifteen years. There are possibly thirty-five additional arson cases that are connected to him. I have been working on these cases for years and I could use some fresh eyes on it. I'm hoping you might be able to see something that I can use to point me in a direction of who this arsonist is."

That was interesting. If he'd been working on catching a single arsonist for fifteen years that meant one of two things. One, either the arsonist was incredibly intelligent, so much so that he was able to operate for so long without ever getting caught. Or two, he didn't exist and Tristan was chasing an invisible man. I didn't know him well enough to know if he was after a ghost or a real person, but either way I couldn't turn him down. He deserved to know the answer and if this arsonist was real, we had to stop him before someone else was killed by him. This time it was one woman, but the next time it could be a whole family, and that wasn't something I could allow to happen.

"I'm always happy to give the Investigative Unit a hand. I can meet you tomorrow at your office, if you want."

"I actually hoped we could meet at my apartment tonight. I know it's short notice."

It was very short notice and I wasn't certain I wanted to go over to his place tonight. I wanted that drink of whiskey. Hell, I wanted five of them, preferably with pizza. The last thing I wanted to do was go over to his place and look through case files of dead people.

And yet, that seemed to be the one thing Tristan really wanted to do.

I could say no. Tell him that I could go by tomorrow and we could look them over. However, I suspected that even if I said tomorrow he would just go home and look through them himself all night.

It was the last thing I wanted to do, but I knew it was the *right* thing to do.

"I'll follow you," I said and nodded.

"I appreciate it," he said, flashing me a small friendly smile.

I hated that a tiny smile from the man brought warmth to my heart and lower. Spending time with Tristan was stupid on my part. Dangerous even. I would have to make sure we got this case wrapped up quickly before I ended up catching feelings for the man. Something I suspected would end about as well as my relationship with Paul. Even if Tristan was gay, he was most likely in the closet like Paul was.

I didn't want to put myself into that position again.

Even if he worked for the Investigations Unit, I knew that it would be just like working on the front lines. The environment would be no different to someone working as a police officer or firefighter. Nope, I refused to be in that position again. I couldn't go through feeling that way any longer. I couldn't sit back and suffer like a dirty secret, and not in the *fun dirty* kind of way. The kind of dirty where if said secret came to light, the only thing I'd be left feeling was shame. I couldn't go through that twice, no matter what.

Tristan headed over to his car and I climbed into my truck. I sat there and looked into the rearview mirror as I waited for when he was ready to head off. As I sat there, I could feel my body getting tired. The exhaustion from the day was setting in now that I was sitting. I was once again questioning if going over to Tristan's place was a good idea tonight. My body and mind were tired and in desperate need of a break, not to mention sleep. Going to Tristain's and looking over old case files was not going to give me the rest I needed, but I did have tomorrow off. With any luck, it would only take a few hours and I could be back home tonight for that drink that I wanted. I could sleep in tomorrow and do all of it with a clear conscience knowing that I had helped Tristan, hopefully, find a lead on his arson case.

I cranked the key and turned my truck on, pulling out onto the road behind Tristan. With any luck, tonight would go smoothly and I would be home before I knew it.

CHAPTER FIVE

Tristan

AS I MADE the drive to my apartment, I couldn't help but start to question if I was making the right call. I had wanted some fresh eyes to go over the past cases and from what I had heard about Hawke, he was a great set of eyes. He was relatively new to the fire department, so he hadn't had time to build a political agenda or deep alliances with anyone. From everything I had been told, he was a man who wanted to help people and had no problem telling someone the truth. I guess I needed that more than anything right now. For someone else to look over these cases and either tell me I was onto something or I was insane. I didn't even know what result I was rooting for.

Maybe my Captain was right. Maybe I was seeing connections that weren't really there because I wanted so desperately to find the man responsible for my parents' death. I didn't know anymore.

I knew the cameras were used in all thirty-five cases that I had discovered so far. I knew that they were from a discontinued line fifteen years ago. I didn't think it was a coincidence that they were present in all of those cases. I knew anyone could purchase them, at least fifteen years ago they could, but what would be the odds of these people having these cameras in their homes without it being connected to the same arsonist?

That was why I needed a new set of eyes. I needed someone to tell me that they believed me. That I was not crazy or seeing things that just didn't matter. I didn't know if Hawke would be my saving grace, but I was really hoping he would be.

Hawke was something else, too. Everyone that I spoke to about him all had nice things to say. A first-class guy who was looking to help people, do something good in this world. He hadn't been in the department for long, but what he'd managed to do in that short time had been impressive.

He was impressive.

I didn't trust people often; it took a lot for me to build a deep level of trust with someone. And I never trusted anyone without knowing them, but for some reason my gut was telling me I could trust Hawke. I wasn't certain I was ready to listen to my gut on that just yet, but I was willing to bring Hawke in and see what he could pick up.

A few investigators had said it was like his parents knew he would be observant, and that was why they named him Hawke. I wasn't too sure how observant Hawke would be, but I was willing to give him a shot. After all, it wasn't like I had anything to lose at this point. Either I found evidence that would allow me to keep investigating these fires with my Captain's permission. Or I didn't find any evidence and I was right back to where I started. I could only go up from here and it was worth the shot.

I knew my Captain would not tolerate it all for much longer. He was already at the point where he wanted to put me on leave for therapy treatment. If that happened there was no telling what could happen to my career. Once you got a report like that in your file, it followed you everywhere you went. Every time I was up for promotion, it would be there. If I were ever being investigated, it would be there and would be used against me. I would become the *unstable investigator* and that was a legal risk waiting to happen. I couldn't let that happen, which meant Hawke was my last chance to find something that I could use as evidence to prove my theory.

When I arrived at my apartment, I parked in the first spot I could find on the street. It wasn't until that moment that I realized I would be having Hawke in my apartment. I didn't have people in my apartment. I didn't have friends. I didn't have coworkers who would come by to drop off files or have coffee.

I liked being alone.

I was good at alone.

When I was alone, I didn't have to try and explain myself. I didn't have to justify my actions. I didn't have to try and explain to anyone why I didn't have photos all over my walls or proper furniture for company. I also didn't have to deal with any of the pitying looks when they saw my boards for my parents' investigation. I hadn't been planning on having Hawke over to my apartment, but it just made sense to meet at my apartment as opposed to my office or a bar. Hopefully, Hawke wouldn't ask too many questions and we could just go over the files.

Letting out a sigh, I admitted to myself there really was nothing I could do about it now. I climbed out of my car and strode over to the entrance of my apartment building. I glanced down the street and saw Hawke's truck pull into another parking spot.

The area that I lived in wasn't the best and I really hoped Hawke wasn't the type to question everything. I didn't need to live in a nice area. I didn't need to have fancy furniture and decorations. I just needed my work and a place to do it in. I was simple in that sense and I was perfectly fine with it. The more people someone had in their life the more distractions they had, and I couldn't afford to have any distractions in my hunt for my parents' killer.

Hawke climbed out of his truck and made the short walk over to me, with a short nod as he approached. I pulled open the front door, letting him enter the building in front of me, and we made our way over to the stairs in silence.

I was relieved when he didn't say anything about the lack of elevator or what the place looked like. I knew the apartment building wasn't the best, but it could have been a lot worse. There were no dirty needles, bugs, or mice in the building, so that was something at least. Maybe that wouldn't seem like much to most people, but to me that was all that mattered. Places like this, the neighbors didn't want to get to know you. They didn't want to make awkward and unnecessary small talk in the hallways. They liked to keep to themselves and that was exactly what I wanted.

When we arrived at my apartment, I unlocked the multiple locks that I had before I walked in and flicked the light on. I knew my living room left a lot to be desired, but the only thing that really mattered was my working boards.

"Are these the cases?" Hawke asked as he eyed the boards.

"I have the individual case files, but yes, they are the cases. Thirty-five of them spanning over twenty-one years. I've been working on them for fifteen years."

"And how long have you been working for the investigative division?"

"Fifteen years. Since I was eighteen."

"Most of these cases are closed. Why are you looking into them?"

I could hear the skepticism in his voice. I couldn't blame him for it. Most had been closed marked accidental. The investigators believed that the fires were started from faulty electrical wires or a space heater. Something that wasn't caused by an individual. My gut told me that they were wrong, though. That all of these cases and possibly more were connected to the same arsonist who killed my parents.

I spoke as I went over to the crime

scene photos that still haunted my nightmares. "They were my parents. The case is still unsolved and when I became an investigator, I started to look into it. The original investigator marked in his report that he found these small hidden cameras throughout different parts of the house." I pointed out the multiple photos of the devices on the board. "He assumed they were security cameras, but they weren't. We never had any. My parents never believed we needed a security system. Most of the time they never locked the door. We lived in a safe neighborhood. The kind of neighborhood where everyone knew everyone. There were never cameras. The investigator never found a cause for the fire, so it's been left as unsolved and sits in the cold case room."

I did everything I could to keep the emotions out of my voice. I didn't want Hawke thinking I was running some type of vendetta. Or that I was the kind of victim who couldn't let it go, who couldn't accept that accidents happened and we all had to find a way to move on.

My Captain had already suggested that my parents most likely purchased the cameras for security and had just never told me so I wouldn't worry or be scared. And maybe they would have purchased something like that without informing me, but I knew my parents. I wasn't a little kid when they'd been killed. I was twelve. I had been old enough to understand the need for a security system. That just wasn't the life we lived.

Someone had started that fire.

Someone had put the cameras in and someone had killed my parents, almost killing me. I wasn't crazy. There was simply no way there could be the same connection in thirty-five cases and for it to be a coincidence. I just couldn't, wouldn't believe that. The odds of that even happening were astronomical. I was right, I knew I was. I just needed someone else to believe it, too.

"I'm sorry about your parents," Hawke said in that pitying tone that I hated.

"Don't. Don't do that. I don't need pity. I don't need that tone and that look in your eyes. The one that says, *'oh that poor guy, can't move on from his parents' death.'* I don't need it and I don't want it. I'm not holding on to something that isn't there. I'm not trying to see patterns that don't exist. I've just hit a wall and I'm hoping a fresh set of eyes will help me see around it."

I didn't do pity and I sure as shit wasn't going take it from him. I didn't know what his life was like, but I did know that he didn't come across to me as someone who understood how much life could suck.

I'd had a perfect life, up until I was twelve when the world decided it was time to swallow me whole. I was still waiting for the gate to open so I could finally leave Hell. It was why I was hunting down this arsonist so strongly. If I could catch him. If I could finally get justice for my parents, myself, and everyone else this man had hurt, then maybe, just maybe, I could find some peace at last. I could finally get out of the hell I had been trapped in since I was twelve years old.

Hawke held his hands up in a mock surrender as he spoke. "Hey, I'm not judging and I sure as shit am not pitying you. I don't know what it's like to lose my parents, especially in something like this. Fuck, I don't even know what it feels like to have parents. I couldn't imagine having them and then losing them like that. I do not pity you, but that doesn't change that I'm sorry you had to lose them. I'm always happy to help, especially if you think this guy has been setting fires for twenty-one years. I don't know how much help I'll be, but I'm always willing to listen."

I couldn't contain the mental sigh that flooded my mind. I shouldn't have snapped at him like that. My emotions were more tightly wound than I'd thought. I was obviously closer to the edge then I'd thought. I knew I needed to get a grip on myself before my Captain saw it too, and I was given a one-way ticket on the Shrink train.

I also picked up on the fact that he'd said he didn't know what it felt like to have parents. I didn't know anything personal about the man but now I couldn't help but wonder what his life had been like.

Did he not know what it felt like to have parents because they were never there?

Did he grow up with a family member or in the foster care system?

Or did he have parents and they were just checked out?

I knew from some kids at school that

they'd had parents who didn't even talk to them for weeks. That always felt so odd to me.

How could your own parents not say anything to you for weeks?

My parents and I had always talked. We talked at breakfast at the table every morning. We talked at dinner at the table every evening. On weekends we would hang out and talk, watch movies together. We were a family that enjoyed spending time together, so anything else always felt so weird to me, and sad.

As much as I wanted to know Hawke's story, I knew now was not the time. I had to focus all of my efforts on solving these cases. Anything other than this case right now was irrelevant and unimportant.

"I'm sorry for snapping at you, that

was unprofessional," I said to try and clear the air.

"It's all good. What makes you think they are all connected?" Hawke asked, keeping his voice even and professional. The air had been cleared and we could get back on track.

"The same cameras that were in my parents' case are in all of these cases. And these are just the ones that have reported about finding the cameras."

"We found cameras at Ms. Rollins' place," Hawke stated as he turned to look at the other crime scene photos.

"Ten of them. All of the cameras can be traced back to the same brand that was discontinued fifteen years ago. Some of the cases the fire appeared to be started from an accident. A lot of them are assumed to be an electrical fire, but the same device that was discovered at Ms. Rollins' home was discovered in twenty of the other cases. I suspect it was also at the other fifteen, but the investigator or firefighters didn't know to look for it. Most people just assume it's part of the electrical panel and ignore it," I explained.

"All of the cases except your parents' were marked accidental and closed. What made your parents' case different?"

"Investigator David Hopkins was one of the good ones. If a fire was caused by an electrical accident, and someone was killed, he went after the last electrician who touched the house. He came from a long line of contractors and it infuriated him that unlicensed electricians worked on people's homes. My parents had an electrician, Skip, in two weeks before the fire. They wanted to update the kitchen lighting. Hopkins brought him back to the house and made him walk through the whole place and looked at everything. When Skip explained what he needed to do to the electrical box to change out the cords, he noticed the device and told Hopkins that he needed to be looking for an arsonist."

"And Hopkins believed him?" Hawke asked, slightly skeptical. Not that I could blame him. Just because one electrician said something didn't belong, that didn't mean he was right.

"Hopkins brought the device to his father, who had been a licensed electrician for thirty plus years. His father said the same thing, that the device would never be used by any electrician, licensed or otherwise."

"Okay, and you said the device can cause the wires to overheat and start a fire. Is that something that anyone can Google?"

"Today, yes, but not twenty-one years ago. I have always suspected that the arsonist had electrical training to be able to make the device. The parts are untraceable, even the parts that aren't fully destroyed."

"What about the houses or the people? Was there anything that connected them to each other?"

"No. Completely different areas of the city, lifestyle, family situation, some were killed and others were badly burned."

That was the frustrating part, because I couldn't find anything that was similar between the cases. The only thing that truly connected them all was the cameras. It was a weak link and I knew that was why my Captain wasn't interested in reopening the cases and telling the city we had a serial arsonist. I needed something more solid. Something that couldn't be explained away by a mere coincidence.

"So the only thing that connects them is the cameras and these devices in the homes they were found in."

"I know it's not much to work with, and I know people assume I am reaching, looking for my parents' killer in every case that I come across, but I find it very odd that these cameras are in so many homes. Homes that friends have said didn't have any security cameras or system in place. I have called every security company in the city and they didn't have any customers under their names. There was no reason for those cameras to be there," I explained.

"Where does their footage go, do you know?"

"The company is no longer around. I have been trying to track down the wholesalers that could have had some left over, but they all distribute to other stores. So far, I haven't been able to get a list of customers or even all of the stores that might still have some in stock. What little information there is about the cameras online, it states that the cameras don't record footage, you can only watch it live. They were popular for doorbell cameras and nanny cams."

"Until new technology showed up on the scene. It makes sense though, that these cameras would still be used.

There's no way to trace them back to a server. And there is no one that has had access to all of the homes?"

"I have checked mail carriers, delivery drivers, friends, coworkers, contractors, the kid that shoveled their driveways. There is no one that had access to all of these homes." And that was beyond frustrating. I knew it wasn't going to be easy, but I had been hoping for something.

"I don't know how much help I'll be, but I do agree with you. It's too much of a coincidence that these outdated cameras are in so many homes. One or two, sure, but not thirty-five. I thought arsonists don't last this long, though?"

It was a huge relief that Hawke was seeing what I was. It only confirmed what I had hoped, that I wasn't losing my mind. I knew we had one hell of a climb ahead of us though, but at least we could make that climb together.

"Typically they only last a few years, five at most before they are caught either by police or by their own fire. It is rare for someone to last twenty-one years. He would have had to have started young or he's in his sixties and still starting fires. It's also possible that he has an apprentice that he's taught his trade to and they have taken up the mantle."

"That's true. They do love to teach and share with each other. But if it is two arsonists, that's going to make finding them even harder."

No truer words. I had never had a pair of arsonists before. Arsonists were narcissists. They only cared about themselves and they never shared trade secrets. That was, until they were more seasoned. When they started to feel like the walls were closing in on them or they were getting too old to keep starting fires, they took on someone young and moldable to teach so they could live out their desires through a patsy. That was my fear, that the man who killed my parents was teaching someone else, and based on the case files, this was a deadly pair and neither of them were going to stop until they were caught. The best I could hope for was that the teacher was dead and we just had to worry about the apprentice. Still, I was hoping this was the work of one arsonist. That would make everything simpler for the investigation and court proceedings should we get that far. Arson was hard enough to prove in court, the last thing we needed was them both trying to pin the fires on the other person.

"The strongest case we have is Ms. Rollins'. It's the newest and the freshest. If we can find something in her case that we can then link to another, we can establish an evidence pattern."

"Let's get started then," Hawke said flashing me an easy smile.

"Pizza?" I asked as I pulled out my phone.

"I never say no to pizza," Hawke said with a playful grin and a wink that made my stomach flip flop and heat fill my veins.

I needed his help to try and find my parents' killer, but now I was starting to second guess spending this much time with him. I was potentially putting myself in a situation that I wasn't going to survive emotionally. It was too late, though. I needed help and so far, Hawke was the only one with an open enough mind to help me. I just had to be careful. I had to keep things professional and not let his perfect smile throw me off my game.

I could do that.

After all, how hard could it be?

CHAPTER SIX

Hawke

"OH MAN, THESE cases are all starting to blur together," I said, feeling weary as I rubbed my burning, overworked eyes for what felt like the hundredth time tonight.

I was used to working long hours. I was used to running off little to no sleep. But what I wasn't used to was working those long hours and then trying to read tiny print for five hours straight right afterward. This was going to be more challenging and exhausting than I had originally anticipated, that was for sure.

We had nothing but the cameras and the devices that were discovered in most of the homes. It should have been enough, but Tristan's Captain wanted something more. He wasn't convinced, not that I could blame him too much. It could be a coincidence that these homes all had the same cameras in them. They could be explained away, and without any survivors any good defense attorney could get them thrown out as evidence. The same could be said for the device. We could have ten electricians that would testify the device was not standard and the defense could have their own electricians who explained it away. We had no suspects, no motives, no connections, nothing that would give us a pattern to present to his Captain to get these cases reopened.

His Captain was going to be another challenge. He wasn't my Captain, but that didn't change that he was a captain and out-ranked the both of us. Even if I didn't work for him directly, I still had to listen to him.

Tristan didn't say that his Captain had ordered him to stand down, but it was implied and we both knew it. His Captain was not looking to have these cases reopened and I knew it was a combination of him believing that Tristan had lost his mind and was chasing ghosts. But he was also worried about the ramifications of reopening these closed cases, cases that were closed as accidental, and having them investigated for arson. It wouldn't stay quiet for long and eventually, the press would get word about it, bringing questions and potentially embarrassment to the department. If Tristan was right, and my gut was telling me he was onto something, it wasn't going to reflect well on the department and that was something the Upper Brass never handled well. It would be nice to say that the Upper Brass wouldn't want to sweep this under the rug, but they would if they could get away with it. They would arrest this arsonist for Ms. Rollins' death and allow the others to remain closed due to accidental fire. No one would be any of the wiser except for the people involved in the investigation.

It was a bit shady, but the Upper Brass were all political-minded people and they focused on making sure the person above them was happy, and at the top of that pyramid was the Mayor. People would think that the Mayor would want to make sure the city was safe, that the people he represented were safe in their homes especially. However, if the crime rate went up while he was in office, it didn't look good for his re-election.

After all, who would want someone in office who would lie and hide things from the people?

"I'm sorry, I know it's getting late and you just worked a twelve hour shift," Tristan said apologetically, his concern and understanding clear in his red-rimmed eyes.

He didn't have anything to be sorry for, though. He didn't ask for this arsonist to be this big of a pain in the ass. Usually, he would have a team helping him, but with his Captain not looking to investigate he was on his own.

Or more accurately, we were on our own.

That was okay though, because I was confident that we would solve this case, one way or another. Even if we couldn't get the arsonist on the other cases, we could get him for Ms. Rollins' case and that would get him put behind bars for life. The other victims would get justice by proxy, which was not ideal, of course, but it was better than nothing. Not very comforting to the surviving victims or the deceased victims' loved ones, but unfortunately justice didn't always come with a straight arrow. Sometimes you had to accept the roundabout option.

"It's fine. I can tell you have been pulling double or triple shifts working on this case, too. It can't be easy on you to have to go through all of this on your own. To repeatedly look at the crime scene photos from your parents' fire."

I couldn't imagine having to go through my parents' file, to see their crime scene photos, to see their charred bodies. I couldn't decide if it made him incredibly strong or incredibly disturbed. He literally had their photos pinned to a board in his living room. He would see it every time he walked into the room or sat on his couch.

The room was another thing. I didn't need to be a therapist to know that he was going through something. There were no personal items in the room. I didn't know if he had anything in his bedroom, but I suspected not. The furniture was old and clearly bought second-hand a very long time ago. The place was small and the area he was living in was one-step above criminal. It felt like someone that didn't know what a home was, which didn't make much sense because from what I'd read about his parents, they came across as loving people. No one had a bad thing to say about any of them, which was rare.

I could relate to him struggling with making a home for himself. When I aged out of the foster care system, I didn't know what to do. I had spent so many years dreaming about having my own place, that when it finally happened I had no idea what to do. I had no idea how to turn an apartment into a home.

I can still remember my first apartment, it was a studio apartment about five hundred square feet in the most disgusting building I had ever been in still to this day. There were mice, cockroaches, and dirty needles everywhere. I woke up with new bug bites every day. At the time though, it was my own personal Heaven, because no one was trying to hurt me. I didn't try to turn it into a home, nor the next five apartments after that.

When I finally got my house that was when I wanted to make it into something real. I wanted to turn it into a home, my first home, and it took me a good couple of years before I finally figured out how to make it a real home.

It seemed like Tristan was going

through that himself. The file never said what happened to him after the fire. I knew he was twelve at the time of the fire, but that was all I knew.

A deep fear spread through my body at the thought that he might have been placed in the foster care system as well. It would explain why he was having a harder time adjusting. It didn't seem like he had many friends. None of the investigators that I had worked with before had ever mentioned him. Keeping to himself was a classic sign that someone grew up in a foster home. Foster homes could get pretty rough and sometimes it was safer to stick to yourself and keep your head down. Now I had more questions and none of them were about any of these case files.

"I'm used to operating with little

sleep," he said with a small shrug as he pulled his sleeves up just slightly.

He wore a long sleeved shirt, but that slight pull was enough for me to be able to see the raised scars that were around his left wrist. Before my mind even registered what I was doing, I reached out and gently took his left wrist in my hand. I felt him flinch for a second at the sudden contact, but he didn't pull his wrist away. I carefully pulled his sleeve up further and I could see the scaring covered his whole left forearm.

"You were there," I said softly as I looked into his eyes. I didn't let go of his wrist though. I wasn't ready to give up the contact for reasons I wasn't prepared to think about.

"There's that tone again," he said softly as well.

I could tell he didn't like pity, not that I was giving him pity right now. I would never pity him. He was one of the strongest men I had ever met. He survived a fire that took the lives of his parents. A fire that odds were he wasn't going to make it out just like his parents never did. And instead of letting that dictate his life and destroy him, he'd dedicated his life to hunting down arsonists. It also made sense why he was so determined to solve his parents' murder. It was almost his.

"You'll never get pity from me, Tris. You're a survivor, the last thing you deserve is pity for it," I said with complete strength to my voice. I was not going to tolerate having him think that I pitied him for any of this. He was a survivor and that made him courageous.

"People don't know. I'd like to keep it that way."

"They won't hear it from me. Can I ask why you kept it a secret?"

It wasn't any of my business and I would completely understand if he didn't want to answer me. It was obviously a very painful night for him physically, mentally, and emotionally. It was probably the worst day of his life and having a constant reminder of it wouldn't have been easy. Knowing that he was there, and not just standing outside in horror as it happened, but actually in the house, it made a lot of sense why he was struggling. Why he lived well below his means; why he didn't have anything personal in this place. He didn't just lose his parents at the age of twelve, he almost lost his own life, and as a reward for surviving he had a scared arm that would always bring up those painful memories.

"I don't like pity and I don't like looks of sympathy. I got it enough when I was in the hospital. When people see it, they look at me with pity and then they ask me what happened. I don't need to tell the story a hundred times. It's just easier to keep it hidden," he answered with a small shrug.

"I get that. You shouldn't have to feel like you have something to hide. You shouldn't have to deal with all of the questions or looks. At the same time, I get why you are hiding it, because people will ask. People are naturally curious and they don't often think twice about asking someone a personal question. It's still not fair to you, though."

I knew from speaking with other fire survivors on this job that oftentimes it was the questions that they were constantly being asked that were the hardest part of recovery. Everyone always looked at the scars. They always assumed what happened. They made up stories in their mind and then they went and asked what happened to see if they were right. Survivors had no choice but to either keep the scars hidden or deal with the looks and questions for the rest of their life. It wasn't fair, but life rarely was. Even still, knowing that it was happening to Tristan, it made me angry. He didn't deserve to go through that level of pain. He didn't deserve the constant reminder and having to always keep it hidden or be subjected to harassment, even if the harassment wasn't malicious intent.

"Life never is. My Captain knows about me being in the fire, but that's it. I know my coworkers could know, they are used to being around people with scars from their investigations. But I don't want to be the investigator who is there because they are chasing their own justice. I don't want them to question my reason for being an investigator."

"Would they really question it? I mean, I know of guys who are firefighters that had been in a fire growing up. It's what made them decide to be a firefighter in the first place. Aren't there other investigators who have been through something similar?"

It wasn't unheard of for there to be a firefighter that had personal experience with a fire before they were on the job. Sometimes it was them in the fire and others it was a loved one that was hurt by a fire. That close call or encounter was what fueled their desire to be a firefighter. To help people survive something that had affected their own life so deeply. I couldn't imagine it would be a problem for the investigator division.

"Maybe. I don't know. It's not something that I have asked around about. I keep things professional, it's easier that way."

"I can understand that. I'm different in that sense. I grew up in the foster care system. I spent eighteen years being distant and trying to keep my nose clean, head down, and just get through each day. When I got out and got my first real job, I wanted to know everything about everyone I worked with. I like building personal connections. I don't have a hundred friends, I have a lot of acquaintances, but the close friends that I have, I know everything about them and the other way around," I said as I ran my thumb along the bottom of his wrist. I really should've let go of his wrist, but I couldn't bring myself to do it. He wasn't pulling away and I took that as a good sign.

"So you're close to the guys at the firehouse?"

"They're my brothers. That was my thing. After being on my own for so long, after not having a family, I wanted one so badly. I went from job to job just trying to find one that would fit and give me that family I was craving. Then I just happened to be in the right place at the right time when a car accident occurred. The one driver was trapped and I stayed with them until the EMT guys and firemen showed up. I remember standing off to the side just watching them work after that. The way they helped the victims. They way they interacted with each other. But at the end, when everyone was taken care of, they had warm smiles on their faces and a few of the guys gave each other a side hug. I could tell they were a family and I wanted that more than anything. I did a drive by at their station a few days later and I fell in love with it. The fear of running into a burning building wasn't enough to keep me away and I signed up that day," I explained, flashing him a warm smile.

"People at work say the firehouses are all like family. I wasn't certain I believed it. It's nice to hear that it's true. I'm happy that you found a home," he offered, returning the smile, but I could also see the longing in his eyes.

Tristan might not be ready to have a home, but he wanted one and that was a good sign. It meant that he still had dreams. That he had the desire to have more in his life than just case files. I was not a therapist in any shape or form, but I knew PTSD when I saw it. I had seen it from veterans and from guys on the job. Fire had a way of bringing trauma and Tristan had gone through a fire that killed his parents. Hell, the house was basically dust by the time the firefighters got it under control. Everything he had would have been destroyed. He had nothing but the memories of his parents and unfortunately, those fade over time.

"I know we just technically met and you have no reason to trust me at all, but if you ever wanted to talk about what happened, I'll always listen. Or if you ever want to not be alone, to just sit with someone in the quiet, I'll be there for that, too."

I knew from my own experiences, both growing up and since being a firefighter, that sometimes people just needed someone to sit with them so they didn't feel alone. It wasn't about opening up and talking about what was bothering them, it was simply about having someone there. I suspected that Tristan didn't have anyone to do that with him.

"I appreciate that. I'm not really good

with people," he admitted, and it surprised me slightly. He worked with people all the time, from coworkers to surviving victims and their loved ones. He didn't come across as someone who didn't like people or interacting with them.

"That surprises me. I didn't get that vibe from you."

"I used to be very social. I had a big family, no siblings, but a lot of cousins and uncles and aunts. They were on my dad's side. Everything was a big deal, holidays, birthdays, even accomplishments, anything to bring everyone together. I had a bunch of friends at school. I was almost never alone."

"And then the fire happened," I stated.

"And then the fire happened. I went from being the fun, popular guy at school to the orphan with the weird looking arm. People who I thought were my friends didn't even come see me in the hospital. The ones who stuck around, they treated me differently, like I was made out of glass. It was just easier to fade everyone out. To keep anyone new at a distance. There's a fine line between being friendly and being dismissive of others. I always try to walk it. Honestly, I don't think I even know how to be social anymore."

"You've been through a lot. You lost your parents and your friends at an age that was pretty vital to your social skills and mental health. It's natural that you would have a harder time with social situations, with being around people and having close friends. We didn't go through the same experiences, but growing up I kept people at a distance, too. I was the orphan kid who couldn't afford new clothes or school lunches. I didn't let people get close to me, either. Sometimes it just takes the right people at the right time to make you come out of your shell again. You said you had a lot of family, what about them? Are they not local?"

Having friends leave when life gets hard was pretty typical at any age, but especially at the young age of twelve. Pre-teens and teenagers were not emotionally and mentally equipped to handle something like what Tristan went through. Though it sounded like he had a lot of family so he wouldn't have been subjected to the foster care system.

HAWKE

"I don't know what happened. One day everyone was there, and the next it was just me and my grandparents. Everyone just... disappeared. Even when I was in the hospital for two months afterward recovering from the burn, no one showed. My grandparents even stopped coming by after two weeks. It was just me and whatever nurse was on duty. We used to go days not saying anything. It was weird and hard at first to adjust to it. I was so used to my parents and how they were. My mom never cared if we made a mess cooking, got flour everywhere. My grandmother though, everything had to be clean and perfect. It felt like a museum compared to a home. I didn't understand it at first, but as I got older I understood that seeing me was a reminder of everything they lost. No one likes to have a reminder of the worst day in their lives staring back at them," he said with a small shrug.

I could understand it. I'd seen it plenty of times in the foster care system. From the kids who were given up because they were a product of rape, to the kids who were given up because their parents were dead and the family couldn't handle it. Unfortunately, when tragedy happens the children can be pushed aside because it's too painful to see the resemblance in them. It wasn't fair, and it often left the children with more trauma they had to work through as adults, but people didn't tend to think about the big picture. All they could see was the small picture in front of them and something had to give. It was hard to know what would have been better for him, to stay with his grandparents who didn't know how to deal with their own loss and trauma, or for him to be given over to foster care. It was a coin toss and there was no way of knowing how it would have ended up.

"I'm sorry. That wasn't fair to you. Loss does things to people and sometimes all they can do is focus on the things they can control. That doesn't make it hurt any less on your end. You have the chance now though, to build your own family. When you're ready, I am sure you will find some great people who would love to be a part of your family."

"Maybe. It's getting late, we should call it a night," he said, and I could see him distancing himself again. We had opened a deep wound tonight and now he needed time to try and close it up again.

"Definitely. Why don't I message you tomorrow and we can pick this up. We could both use some sleep and we might see something tomorrow that we missed," I said as I pulled my hand back and stood up.

I could see the raw pain in his eyes as he fought to get it back under control. He needed some time and space to be alone and that was exactly what I was going to give him. Tomorrow, I could come back over and we could keep pushing through the case files. I hoped we would find something that we could use. If this dragged on for too long our arsonist could hit another home and that was the last thing we both wanted.

CHAPTER SEVEN

Tristan

I DON'T KNOW what I had been thinking, opening up to Hawke like that. I didn't talk about my past. I didn't talk about my childhood, not the fire or anything that came after it. It wasn't like I was ashamed of any of it; I just didn't want to talk about it. I didn't want to remember what happened in great detail. Not that I couldn't recall every single second of the horror from that night. It would be impossible for me to forget what happened to me, what had been stolen from me.

I would have loved to forget.

Sometimes, I thought it would have been better if I'd had some type of head trauma or if I had forced the memories into the dark recesses of my mind to protect myself. I had heard it plenty of times from surviving victims that they just wished they could remember what happened. That not remembering, not knowing, was making them go crazy from the unknown of it all. For me though, all I wanted to do was forget. I wanted to forget what the smell of burning flesh smelled like. I wanted to forget what it felt like to look at my parents' bedroom and know that there was nothing I could do to help them. I wanted to forget what it felt like to have my chest being tight and on fire at the same time as I fought for each breath in the thick black smoke. I wanted to forget everything, but I couldn't.

I remembered that night in vivid detail, so much so that I didn't even need the crime scene photos to help me recall even the smallest details. It seemed fitting that I would remember the night that changed my life forever. A night that destroyed everything that I knew of family, friends, and myself.

I didn't talk about it, so why the hell did I tell Hawke so much about it. I never talked about my time in the hospital or what happened to my friends and family. I kept that to myself and whenever someone asked about it, I would just smile and say they were great. That I couldn't have recovered without them. It was a lie, but I knew that's what people wanted to hear. They didn't truly want to know what my life was like afterward. They were only being socially polite by asking.

It was the same thing as a stranger asking how you were doing. You never tell them that your roof leaks and you just lost your job. You tell them you are fine and move on. That's what I should have done with Hawke, but for some reason my mouth didn't listen to my brain.

Talking with Hawke felt like talking with an old friend. One that knew you growing up and knew all of your secrets. At the same time, he felt like a hypnotist.

HAWKE

The calm sound of his voice put me in this weird trance where all I wanted to do was open and share my deepest and darkest secrets. It was very odd and not like me at all. I wasn't certain how I felt about it.

"Jesus, fuck," I said as I rubbed my hands over my face.

I was exhausted and I knew I needed to sleep. I was barely sleeping anymore and I knew it was going to make my mind sluggish and I could potentially miss something that I usually wouldn't. I needed some serious sleep, but I honestly had no idea how I was going to accomplish that tonight.

My sleep patterns had always gone up and down. I could go months without a single problem and then my insomnia would act up and I was back to sleeping a few hours every couple of days.

I knew a therapist would tell me it was PTSD from unresolved traumatic issues from the fire. That being a fire investigator was only making it worse and the best course of action for my mental and emotional well being would be to quit. It was why I didn't want to be ordered to see the company Shrink. I knew what he would say and the very last thing I needed was it on record that I was a walking ticking time bomb that the fire department needed to get rid of. I knew this job was hard, I knew that going in, but I had made the decision to risk everything just to find justice for my parents. I was not about to let anything stop me and that was more true today than it had been when I'd first started.

Letting out a sigh, I stumbled to my

feet and made my way into my bedroom. I doubted I would be able to sleep for very long before the nightmares would hit, but I had to give it a shot at least. It was something I was trying to make a habit of doing. Trying to sleep even when I knew my mind would not allow me to. I figured if I tried and it didn't work, then I could give myself a break with knowing that I had at least tried and didn't just give up right away. It was a battle, but I felt better knowing that I had at least shown up to the battle and tried to come through on the other side.

I quickly got ready for bed and turned my bedside lamp on. It was dim enough that it wouldn't keep me awake, but it was bright enough to allow me to see the room.

Yet another reason why I couldn't

date anyone.

No man would be able to understand that I couldn't sleep in the dark, that I was like a child in need of a nightlight. It wasn't sexy and it certainly wouldn't make a man want to spend more time with me. It definitely didn't make them want to date me. Not that I was looking for a date anyway.

I crawled into bed and tried to get my body to relax as I closed my eyes. With some luck tonight, the exhaustion that was wreaking havoc on my body would finally allow me to fall into a deep sleep.

***

The hot water washed over me, cascading down my body. I had my head tilted down, but my eyes were closed to prevent any water droplets from getting into my eyes. My left hand was pressed flat against the shower wall, but not even now did the cool tile disrupt my moment of peace. I moaned as a wave of pleasure shot up my spine. My right hand worked away at my hard dick.

It wasn't often I would feel the need to pleasure myself, but when I woke up this morning with a raging hard on, I couldn't ignore it. I had tried, but it wouldn't go back down. The four hours that I had managed to sleep for were filled with dreams. I was used to having nightmares or weird dreams, it was very common for me. What wasn't common was for me to have multiple sex dreams about someone. I didn't even wake up in between, they just flowed from one scenario to another, each one getting hotter than the last. Hawke was haunting me, but instead of him flickering my lights, he was bringing me to new heights in pleasure.

I couldn't stop thinking about the dreams. I couldn't stop seeing it. They played behind my eyes with perfect clarity. I could remember every single touch, every press of his lips on my skin, every single time he slid into me. The way his mouth felt wrapped around my dick. It all felt so real, as if we had already done it and my body was remembering our time together.

Only, we had barely touched and certainly nothing sexual. There was no reason for my body to be reacting this way. I had more self-control over my libido than this, and yet here I was jerking off for the third time in the past hour and it still didn't feel like enough. I hadn't even felt like this when I hit puberty.

I had never been a very sexual person. I could easily go years without sex, and I had without a second thought about it. I had never felt like this before. No matter how many times I came, I still needed more, I wasn't sated and I had no idea how to be.

I let out a deep moan as I came once again. Not much came out and I was pretty certain the well was dry at this point. I placed my forehead against the shower wall and fought to even out my breathing. The heat from the water was starting to go to my head and I was feeling very light headed. I knew I needed to get out, but I just needed a second to catch my breath before I could move. I was supposed to be seeing Hawke later on today and now I had no idea how I was going to pull this off.

Would I get hard by just seeing him?

Would seeing him pull all of my dreams from last night back into my head?

I couldn't afford to be distracted, not when the best chance of catching my parents' killer had presented itself. I needed to focus all of my attention on getting this arsonist off the streets and in jail where he belonged.

Letting out a sigh, I pushed myself up and reached down to turn the water off. I looked down and saw that my dick was already half-hard again and I couldn't help the scowl that touched my face.

"Fuck off," I muttered, before I climbed out of the shower and grabbed one of my towels.

I was ignoring my dick. It had had

enough fun for the next few months. I was stronger than this and not about to spend anymore time indulging in something as frivolous as self-pleasure.

After quickly drying off, I made my way into my bedroom to get dressed. I didn't have any plans of going anywhere today. I didn't have work officially, so there was no need for a suit. I grabbed a pair of blue jeans and a black t-shirt. Just as I finished getting dressed my cell phone went off. Instantly, my heartbeat increased and I hoped that it was Hawke that was calling me.

It was ridiculous, because there was no need for him to call me. I had to get a grip on myself. I wasn't going to let a pretty face disrupt my life. He wasn't the first good looking guy that I'd had to work with. I had to focus and stop thinking of him like some lovesick teenager.

I picked up my phone and saw that it was work. I already knew what this was going to be about. There was only one reason I would be called on my day off.

"Investigator Cole," I said, already going over to my closet to pull out a change of clothes.

"Engine fifty-seven is calling for an investigator. Three dead in a fire at 467 Wilton Street. They found an electrical device in the electrical panel. You have an open case with the same device," the dispatcher said.

Every fire investigation dispatcher had access to all open cases. They didn't have the specifics, but they could see the investigator's name and the cause of the fire. It was designed that way so if there was an arsonist operating in town, they could easily get the case files over to the right investigator. It wasn't perfect, there had been plenty of overlap with similar signatures and MOs, but for the most part it helped to keep things organized.

"I'm on my way," I said, before I ended the call.

Letting out a sigh, I pulled up Hawke's number and called him. I wasn't certain if he would be awake or not. We had wrapped up late and I knew he still had to drive home. I was hoping that he would be awake and already have had a cup of coffee. After three rings a very groggy voice answering told me that I had indeed woken him up.

"Colton."

"It's Tristan. I am sorry to wake you up. I just thought I would let you know that there was another fire at 467 Wilton Street. There's three dead, and they found the same device in the electrical panel. I'm heading out now."

"Shit. He just struck yesterday. The gap in between fires was months apart," Hawke said, sounding more awake now. I could hear rustling and I knew he was getting up.

"I know. It could be a coincidence, but I doubt it. I'm getting ready to head out now. I'll have more information once I arrive on scene."

"What firehouse was it?"

"I don't know. The dispatcher said it was Engine Fifty-Seven on scene."

"All right, I know one of their guys, I'll give him a call and get him to start looking for any cameras in the walls."

"I appreciate it. I'm guessing I'll see

you there."

"I'll be there within twenty."

"See you then." I said, before I ended the call.

I couldn't help but stand there and look down at the black screen on my phone. More often than not when I got the call to head to a fire to investigate, I would feel anxious in a sense. Well, more like anxious dread. I didn't like seeing the dead bodies, and each fire I had to investigate, I knew it would be devastating to a good number of people, even if no one had died.

This time around though, there was no dread, no anxiety. In its place was a warmth at knowing that I would be getting to see Hawke sooner than I had been expecting.

That feeling sickened me for two

reasons. The first, I didn't want to look forward to seeing anyone. I wanted to go through life on my own without having to deal with someone else. I didn't want to have to deal with more disappointment and not being good enough for someone else's love. The second, I was looking forward to going to a fire where three people were dead, just so I could see a man.

It was sick and wrong.

I needed to get my head back on track. I wasn't going to let Hawke come into my life and ruin everything I had worked so hard for. I wasn't going to let him tear down all of the walls I had carefully constructed around my heart and mind.

With that determination, I quickly got changed and grabbed my wallet, phone, keys, and badge before I headed out. I had an arsonist to catch and I was not going to let him slip through my fingers again. Too much was riding on finding him, on stopping him, and now I had another three reasons to find him. The body count was climbing and if we didn't stop him soon, he was going to lose all control and there was no telling how many lives would pay for my shortcomings.

CHAPTER EIGHT

Hawke

I PARKED IN the first spot I could find around the crime scene. There was police tape up to block off the main area and keep any cars from passing through. Engine Fifty-Seven was still there and I knew they were going to be there for the next few hours as they worked their way through the destruction. I couldn't see the house clearly, but I could see the top of it and it was a very usual sight for me. The house was still standing so I had to give the guys credit, they'd worked hard to keep the house and to prevent the fire from jumping to one of the nearby homes.

It was not as easy as people thought it was to keep a fire under control, especially when the houses were so close together. One gust of wind in the wrong direction and it could blow the embers into the roof of the nearby house. Most people wouldn't think embers would be enough to start a fire, but with roofing materials, that was all it could take. Roofs weren't designed to prevent fire, they were designed to prevent water from getting into your house. Shingles could very easily catch fire, especially if they were old and dried out. The rubber matting underneath that is designed as a water barrier became a deadly accelerant when it melted. It was a dance that every firefighter had to perform when we were working with houses very close together. A dance we didn't always accomplish.

I got out and made my way toward the crime scene tape. I held up my badge as I ducked under the tape. I scanned the area to try and see if I could find Tristan. I doubted I'd beat him here but anything was possible.

I saw the Coroner's van was still here and I knew that the crime scene would be too busy inside taking photos of the bodies before they could be moved. I still didn't know more than what little Tristan had told me on the phone. I knew there were three dead, but I had no idea if they were adults, children, or a mix of both.

I was hoping they were adults.

It would be terrible for three adults to lose their lives, but it was worse when it was children. Children dying in a fire was a whole new horror, one I was never able to handle. No firefighter could handle the death of a child, especially in a fire. The fear of being trapped in a fire was traumatic on every level, but to know that a child had faced that fear all alone, it was unspeakable.

I still couldn't believe that Tristan had gone through that himself. That at twelve years old he'd lost his parents and almost his own life in a fire that was set by an unknown male. He didn't have closure and I wanted that for him. I wanted to be able to help him heal from the open wound. I knew he wasn't fully healed. I could see it in his eyes. He was fighting and trying to be okay, but I could see it. He needed his parents' killer caught. He needed it in order for him to finally heal and move on in his life. He was standing still and it wouldn't get better until he could close that part of his past and start looking toward the future.

I headed inside the house and started to look for Tristan. It didn't take me very long before I found him. He was talking to Jase, the guy that I had called to search for the cameras. We went through the Fire Academy together and I knew he was a good guy. We would often grab a beer when we could. We tended to work opposite shifts though, so it wasn't very often we could meet up and share war stories.

I paused for a moment as I gazed at Tristan and my heart skipped a beat. Even his profile called to me, to my heart, and I had yet to figure out why.

I'd had plenty of dreams last night, wonderful and sinful dreams of the man. I was no stranger to sexy dreams. I was a man, after all, with a very healthy sex drive. However, the dreams from last night had felt so real. They felt more like memories, but I knew that wasn't even possible.

This morning I'd tried to dismiss it as a fluke. Convinced myself that I must have been around him at some point on a case and that was why he felt so familiar, why I was so immediately and intensely attracted to him. But I could no longer fool myself. I couldn't ignore how familiar he felt any longer.

I knew most people didn't believe in soul mates, but I did. I believed wholeheartedly that when people died they eventually were reborn and they met the same people they had in their past lives, especially the person they were destined to be with. I knew it sounded silly, like a hopeless romantic, but I truly believed it.

I had come across people who are some of my best friends now, all because they felt so familiar to me when I'd met them for what I knew was the first time. There was just a gut instinct that drew me to them, convinced me they belonged in my life.

And that was just it, the same gut instinct had kicked in and I realized at that moment that Tristan felt like an old love. It felt like my body knew him on a deeper level and I needed to take that into account. I simply couldn't ignore it anymore. I didn't want to, truth be told.

I *needed* to know more of this man.

The trick was I had to be very careful. I had to tread carefully with this because I had no idea if he was gay and if he was, I didn't know if he was out. I couldn't go through another relationship with a man who was in the closet. I couldn't handle being a dirty secret again. It had destroyed parts of my soul, parts that I was just starting to get back, and I couldn't endure it again. Not even if that meant that I would miss out on the chance to be with Tristan. I had to do what was right for me and being kept as a secret wasn't a healthy lifestyle for me.

Even if Tristan was gay and out, that didn't mean there wouldn't be obstacles. He was clearly struggling with the traumatic experiences of his life. That was made very clear to me after learning about his family and friends after the fire. He was undoubtedly used to being on his own and having something or someone there to be strong for him, to allow him to be vulnerable and not strong all the time, to help him through the pain and heartache, that entire concept was completely foreign to him. He wasn't going to let his walls down very easily and it was going to take some serious work to break through them. However, even knowing all of that, my heart was still telling me it would all be worth it.

That the work and potential

frustration would be worth it.

I could see the pain in his eyes as we talked last night, but I could also see a longing for more. He *needed* more. He wanted to be happy and healthy, he wanted to move past his rocky history and get on with living, and as long as that spark for life was still in his eyes, that was all the hope I needed.

I waited until Tristan gave a nod to Jase and then Jase turned and strolled off to speak with some of the other guys. Tristan turned toward me and our eyes locked. I could have sworn I saw a flash of heat briefly go across his eyes before they were locked down once again. I made my way over to him, flashing him with a warm smile as I spoke.

"Morning. What do we know?"

"Engine Fifty-Seven arrived on scene

just after eight this morning. The house was already consumed in flames. Local police were evacuating the nearby homes. Most were empty though, with people having to get to work. Homeowner is Shelby Lewis, thirty-seven with two kids. A ten year old boy named Chris and an eight year old girl named Katie. Local police reached out to next of kin, Shelby's mother, Grace. She informed them that Shelby and the kids had been home for the past two days, all were sick from the flu. Grace was supposed to spend the night on the couch, but her daughter told her that she was feeling better and she didn't need to. Grace is a mess and currently blaming herself, believing that if she'd stayed she would have woken up in time to save her daughter and grandchildren."

"Fuck," I said as I closed my eyes for a second to calm my emotions down.

It was bad enough when it was children, but to know that they were supposed to be safe tucked away in their beds. They were sick and just staying home from school. If they hadn't been sick, they most likely would have been up and getting ready for school. They would have noticed the fire before it became overwhelming.

"They never made it out of their beds. Engine Fifty-Seven didn't initially suspect arson, but when they started to do their walk through while they waited on the Coroner, they noticed that every smoke detector in the house had their batteries pulled. An officer asked Grace about it and she was adamant that they were functioning. She said two weeks ago she had to personally change the one in the kitchen because it wouldn't stop beeping. She said her daughter was very careful with anything that could start a fire. She didn't have candles, no incense burners, she didn't have curling irons, or space heaters. Her biggest fear was a fire starting. She didn't even use the built-in electric fireplace that came with the house. She even had extra smoke detectors installed in each of the kids' bedrooms."

"Why the paranoia?"

It was common for people to be afraid of fires. I had come across lots of people who made sure there were no accelerants or open flames in their house. I knew plenty of people who'd switched their gas stove out for an electric one. It wasn't that uncommon.

But it was not common for people to go to the extreme by adding more smoke detectors in the house. To not even want to risk a curling iron being left on. There had to be a story there.

"They used to live in Texas, her husband was a firefighter. According to Grace, he was very paranoid about anything that could start a fire. He had twenty years on the job and that paranoia got worse after they had children. He died seven years ago in an industrial fire that took out him and eight others before they were able to get it under control. Shelby and the kids all moved back here to get help from her mother. According to Grace, Shelby became terrified of fire after that. She said she was never the same again. She wouldn't even park her car in the garage in case a fire started and the gas tank blew."

"Okay, so she had a reason to be paranoid. It also works in our favor, though. We've both seen it where people pull the batteries out of their smoke detectors, especially the one by the kitchen. But someone that paranoid, they don't pull all of the batteries from their smoke detectors. She would have had extra batteries for when they died. Someone had to have physically pulled them, but the question is when. If they have been home sick for the past two days, they wouldn't have had anyone coming in to do any work on the house. And they wouldn't have been able to get access to every room."

"Exactly. They had to have been here before they were sick, but within the past two weeks since Grace changed the batteries in the kitchen detector. They would have also had to have been here within the window for the electrical device to be planted in the electrical panel for it to go off at the right time."

"That is what I don't understand. There's no timer on it, so how does our guy know when it will cause a fire and if someone will be in the house when it happens?"

That's what was bothering me. There was no guarantee he would ever get someone in the house when the device started the fire. There were no timers on the device. There was nothing that would indicate he held any control over when a fire would start.

So how was he able to time it right to get victims?

"I don't know. I think there is more to the device then we can see. The ones we have been able to recover have been pretty much melted into nothing. My guess is there is some type of coding, or liquid that he uses as a timer. As it gets hotter the coding or the liquid starts the fire once it reaches a specific temperature. If he knew the flash point of the materials he uses, he would be able to roughly time when a fire would occur."

"Best way to do that is to practice. Maybe we should be looking for smaller fires that were nothing. Fires that didn't even warrant a call to the investigation unit."

He had to have started somewhere and if he needed to perfect his device, he had to practice with it. He would have to have used it in a real setting and timed how long it took to get the right combination down.

"That's a good idea," Tristan said as Jase walked back over to us.

"We found this in the little girl's room," he said as he handed a small black rectangular device over to Tristan.

"Where in the room?" I asked.

"Across from the bed in the corner," Jase answered.

"It's a camera," Tristan said as he looked at the device closer.

"Like a nanny cam or is someone watching this little girl?" Jase asked, both disgusted and angry. I couldn't blame him, there was really nothing good that could come from a camera in a little girl's room.

"Depends on if there are more

cameras all around the house," Tristan answered.

"We're looking in every room. I'll let you know if we find others," Jase said with a nod before he headed off.

"That one doesn't look like the other cameras from previous fires," I stated what I knew we were both thinking.

"I know, but it can't be a coincidence. If there are more cameras in the house, then it has to be the same guy. He must have made a change for some reason."

"Thirty-five fires, each with ten cameras, that's three hundred and fifty cameras. That's a lot of cameras that are no longer being made. Maybe he finally ran out and couldn't get anymore," I suggested.

The cameras were fifteen years old. There couldn't have been that many left out in the world. Even if they didn't get sold, most places would have tossed them as dead inventory. They would take the loss, because they could use the space for items that would sell. It worked out better for them. This guy couldn't have that many of these cameras left and eventually, he would have had to make the change.

"It could explain why he hit so quickly after the last time. He wanted to test out the new equipment. I'll send it to the crime lab and see if they can determine what brand it is. He wouldn't have ordered them online. That would leave an address, name, and a credit card number. He would have wanted to get them in person and paid with cash. We might luck out on security footage at the stores if they are willing to give it over without a warrant."

"They might have an IP address that they feed the footage to. Would he have really stuck so soon just to test out some cameras? Wouldn't it have made sense for him to do a controlled burn with them somewhere instead of risking them failing?"

It made more sense for him to do a controlled burn on a piece of land with a shed or something than an actual house. There was no telling how well the cameras worked under that level of heat. I couldn't imagine an arsonist wanting to risk missing out on watching their work live in action.

"You're assuming he would have a place to do that. Most people don't have the land to build a house to do a controlled burn. This camera isn't as badly burnt as the previous ones. They must have a higher heat level tolerance. That means they would have worked longer for him. Whether this was a test or not, they definitely passed and that doesn't bode well for us."

"How so?" I asked, slightly confused. I would have figured the camera being in better shape was a good thing. We might be able to track it down to a store and find this asshole.

"Because arsonists are compulsive. They have to burn things, they have to start fires. In the beginning they do it in different ways, trying to determine what way made them feel the best. Like drug addicts trying different drugs until they find the one that gives them the best high. These cameras, it's like going from black tar heroin to china white heroin.

He's feeling a whole new high, most likely the best high he's felt since his very first fire. He's going to be chasing that even more now."

"That works in our favor though, doesn't it? He's chasing that high, he's not as careful and he slips up. This could be the house that catches him. This could be his mistake."

I knew from volunteering at soup kitchens and community centers, that drug addicts who were chasing their high often got sloppy. The more desperate they were for that high, the more erratic they became and the more mistakes they made. If our guy was desperately chasing the high he got from this fire, he might make a mistake. He might have made a mistake with how soon he hit this house. I couldn't imagine he had enough time to plan everything out this time around. Not when he usually goes a few months in between fires.

"It's very likely. We need to dig into Shelby's life. It's possible he has been here before. I'll get the camera to the crime lab. Why don't you search the database and see if there are any small fires that could fit with our guy. I will reach out to a cop friend of mine for the intel on Shelby."

"Sounds good. Meet at your place?"

"Um... yeah, okay."

He didn't sound too sure and I couldn't help but wonder if there was a hint of a blush touching his cheeks or if it was simply the heat of the day making them ruddy. I quickly dismissed it, not wanting to let my mind get away from me. We had to focus on finding this arsonist before someone else got killed. Once he was arrested, then I could always entertain the idea of being with Tristan in a romantic capacity. I still had no idea if he was interested in guys or not, maybe I would need to try and slip it into the conversation somehow. For now, we had an arsonist to catch with a body count going up.

I gave him a nod before I headed out. I was hoping that I would be able to find an older fire that would have something we could use to connect to our guy. Arsonists get better with age and experience, if we could find our guy from when he first started out, we might be able to nail him. Arson had a statute of limitations for ten years, but a death in a fire counted as murder, and there was no time limit on that. Every victim that this man had killed, injured, or destroyed their lives, would still be able to get justice. Now we just needed to find him.

CHAPTER NINE

Tristan

AFTER GETTING BACK into my car, I quickly pulled out my phone and placed a call to Detective Jonah West. I had come across him a few times professionally and I liked how he was a straight shooter and that he cared about people.

Some detectives that I had worked

with in the past only cared about their own cases, and even that might be a stretch. They didn't want to take on more cases and they held zero interest in helping with a fire investigation. Most detectives wanted cases that were easy and quick to close, and if there was one thing about arson, it was a long and tedious process to investigate. The fire destroys evidence and any that might be left behind gets destroyed by the firefighters. Most detectives tended to avoid getting a fire case. I'd even seen some trade cases just to get rid of their arson case.

"Detective West," he said, picking up after three rings.

"Detective West, it's Fire Investigator Cole. Do you have a moment to talk?"

"I always have a moment for you,

Tristan. How have you been?" Detective West said, his voice warm and welcoming.

"I have been well, thank you. I caught a serial arson case with multiple bodies on his tally. The most recent is a single mother of two young children. All three are dead. They never made it out of their beds."

"I'm sorry. What do you need?" he asked, more than willing to help. It was one of the reasons why I would reach out to him when I needed some police help.

"I think my arsonist finally made a mistake in picking this victim. He just hit yesterday and generally he has a cooling off period of months, but he hit the next house within twenty-four hours of the last fire. I think he knew her. She was paranoid about fires, her husband was a firefighter in Texas and he was killed seven years ago in a fire. My victim had installed extra smoke detectors in her house, but every single battery was removed before the fire was started."

"So he's been in the house. Any work done on the house recently?"

"Not that the mother of the victim knew about. I got the impression that they were very close. The victim moved back from Texas after her husband's death. I have the report from the officer who spoke with the victim's mother. According to her, my victim was focused on her career and her children. She didn't date. She wasn't ready and didn't know how her children would feel about it. She worked at a marketing firm, BizBeep."

"What's her name?"

"Shelby Lewis, thirty-seven. Kids were Chris, a ten year old boy, and Katie, an eight year old girl. They were home the past couple of days all sick with the flu."

"All right, I'll dig into her and see what I can find."

"I really appreciate the help."

"Always. I'll be in touch in a bit."

"Thanks," I said, and ended the call.

With Detective West looking into Shelby and her life, I was hoping he would be able to find someone who was around that we could connect to Rollins' house or her life. We needed something that connected both homes, because I found it hard to believe that this hit was completely random. He had to have been in their homes to set up the cameras, plant the device in the electrical panel, and for him to know that Shelby had extra smoke detectors that would have ruined his plans.

That didn't scream random to me at all.

This man was in both of their lives. He was either older and responsible for the previous fires, or he was younger and working as an apprentice to the original arsonist that started the fire at my parents' home. I wasn't certain which option it would be. Neither one would be common, but it was the only working theory I had. I couldn't see it being a coincidence that these cameras were used in all of these fires and it wasn't connected. Even Hawke found it hard to believe, which only helped to make me feel more confident in my theory.

With any luck Detective West would be able to find us someone that we could dig into and get him caught before he strikes again.

I cranked the ignition on my car, shifted it into gear, and started to make my way to the crime lab. I needed to get the camera into the hands of a professional and find out everything I could about it. And maybe, just maybe, it would be more traceable than the previous cameras.

***

I made my way through the crime lab to the Digital Forensic Division. I had been there a few times, but it wasn't very often I needed to see Hank. He was the best Digital Forensic Expert I had ever dealt with and often helped me with the previous arson cases that involved the cameras. He didn't tell me I was crazy or seeing things. He just focused on the evidence and didn't speculate on the case at all.

I enjoyed that part.

Sometimes forensic experts wanted to get involved in the case. They wanted to follow it until there was an arrest and conviction. It wasn't a bad thing exactly, but I didn't appreciate someone questioning me the whole time. There was such a thing as too many cooks in the kitchen and often the forensic experts believed they were the only cook who mattered.

Hank wasn't like that. He had enough on his plate so he was more than happy to examine the evidence and then classify his work as complete before moving on to the next file. It was a good part of why we got along so well.

HAWKE

I knocked on the glass door to his lab to alert him to my presence before I turned the knob and opened the door. I strolled in quietly so I didn't disturb his concentration and waited patiently beside his desk. I knew he'd acknowledge me when he was ready. We'd been through the same cycle a few times, after all.

He was staring at a computer screen, and I could see he was reviewing footage from someone's security camera. He was always busy and I hated interrupting him, but it was important and I knew he wouldn't mind too much.

"Cole, tell me this is quick," Hank said, and I could hear the tension in his voice.

I didn't know what he was working on, but I could tell by the stress lines around his eyes that he was working on something major and time consuming. Whatever the case he was working on, it must have been footage heavy. I knew there had been plenty of cases where he had to comb through months' worth of security footage to try and find suspects and evidence. Hank often got headaches from spending hours staring at a computer screen without breaks. One of the major downfalls of the job, and his determination to be one of the best at it only added to the issue. Once he got started he was like a dog with a bone and wouldn't quit until he'd found what he needed.

Most people thought being a digital forensic analyst would be and easy job, but it was a lot of work and brutal on the eyes. One small miss and it could mean the difference between either finding or missing critical evidence in a case.

"I hope so. I have a new camera that was found at a crime scene. MO is the same as the arsonist that I have been chasing, but he changed up the cameras. I was hoping you would be able to tell me more about it," I said as I held up the clear plastic evidence bag with the camera inside of it.

He let out a small sigh before he held out his hand and I passed the bag over to him. I wasn't sure if he liked me or not. It was hard to tell with him. He was always professional, but he didn't do the whole small talk, social thing like most of the experts here did. He also didn't go on rants to prove how smart he was, another common trait in this building.

I knew a lot of the people who worked here were highly intelligent nerds and didn't have much experience in the way of normal social interactions with average people. So I never took it personally when they felt the need to over explain something technical. I never cared to hear about all the technical tests they did on whatever piece of evidence they had from one of my cases, but I dealt with their need to explain anyway. I didn't need to hear about the process to get there, I just needed to see the results. Hank understood that and it made me respect him even more.

I stayed quiet while he worked away. I knew if this was going to take a whole lot longer he would have shooed me away and told me to come back later. The fact that he hadn't told me to leave meant that he wouldn't have to do extensive tests on it. The camera was in a bit better shape then the previous ones I'd brought him to review and I suspected that was just due to the advancement in the materials being used for cameras now. Even plastic has come a long way in the last twenty years. It was roughly thirty minutes later when he finally peered up at me again.

"This one is newer. Model Z by Giget; made within the past three years. It's very popular in the private detective circle, but it has also been used as a nanny cam and pet camera. People don't tend to use them for home security, though, because the mount that comes with them doesn't last very long. These kind are designed to be used for short periods of time and usually placed in some sort of housing or container as opposed to being mounted on a door or a wall."

"Okay, how does it work?"

"A person can watch these feeds live, but they also connect to their own private server. When someone purchases them, they also purchase a server that will store the data on it. The server does not connect to the Internet, which is why it's popular with PIs. They don't have to worry about someone hacking their files. It's done all remotely, but the owner does have to activate the camera and connect them wirelessly to the server. They'd have to do that online through the camera's app, either on a computer, tablet, or a smartphone."

"And how far can the server be from the cameras?"

I was very interested in the private server. If we could find a suspect we could get a warrant to try and find the server. We might not be able to link him to all of the cases, or even my parent's case, but we could at least get him in jail for three counts of murder, a life sentence, and it would at least get him off of the streets.

"To make sure the connection stays, typically the owner wouldn't go further than two miles from the house. Any further and they would risk the connection fading in and out. It's bluetooth connected, so it doesn't give them too much leeway."

Two miles, which meant this time around he had to be in a vehicle or close by somewhere in order to watch the feeds. We could pull street cameras and see if we could find a car that we could connect to a suspect. We would have to run the license plates of any car that had been hanging around too long, which could be a few, but if it meant possibly finding the bastard then it was more than worth it.

"And I'm assuming this server is a black box?"

"Yes, like a portable hard drive. They will most likely have a password on it."

That was a given. "How popular is popular?"

I was almost afraid of what his answer would be. If private detectives were using it, I knew that meant there could be tens of thousands of people who had purchased them. Private detectives were just as talkative as normal cops. They all liked to share trade secrets and give advice on the newest tech to make the job easier. There was no telling how many stores sold them and their customer lists.

"Millions are made a year. They're cheap and they have a fairly decent video quality to them. But, I was able to extract the serial number and traced it back to one store. Spy Guy." He said the name of the store with a small smirk turning up the corners of his lips and I knew he was proud of himself.

That was why I loved Hank. He knew how to get results and he could do it fast. I had never been able to get a serial number on any of the cameras before. They were too melted to ever be able to get anything off of them. I now had a store, a single store, where I could potentially get security footage from and a customer list. That could be the break I needed, the intel that finally gave me a real suspect that I could dig into.

Shelby Lewis was going to be this arsonist's biggest mistake and I was going to make sure of it.

"Thank you Hank," I said, flashing him a warm, grateful smile.

"Go get this son of a bitch," Hank said, before he swung back to stare into the computer monitor he had been working on when I came in.

I headed out of the building and made my way back down to my car with a new pep in my step. I could feel my body tingling with excitement. I was getting somewhere. I was finally getting closer. I could almost taste it now.

The second I slid into my car I hit the browser and pulled up Spy Guy on my phone to find its location. It was a good twenty minutes away, but it was open and that was all that I needed. It was owned by Seth Rogers, and based on the reviews it was a good place with a very helpful owner. I hoped like hell that was true and Mr. Rogers was more than willing to cooperate without making me get a warrant.

I tossed my phone down on the passenger seat and cranked the engine with a smile on my face. Pulling out into traffic, I headed off for Spy Guy.

***

Damn it!

Of course he wasn't going to play ball. Nothing was ever easy. I finally had a real break and Mr. Rogers didn't feel comfortable violating his customer's privacy by allowing me to have access to his security footage or customer list. As if his customers were real spies and not a bunch of middle-aged men following people for a living.

The gadgets in his store were all geared toward catering to the lifestyle of James Bond. Mr. Rogers had found a way to make a very good living by playing into the compulsion that his customers had about being real life spies. I would hate to see the private detectives who shopped at that store. Their hourly fee must be insanely high, not to mention how they likely preferred to handle contact with their clients. I would never understand some people.

Either way, I wasn't getting what I needed without a warrant. Thankfully, that would be easy enough with what

Hank had found on the camera. I grabbed my phone and rang our Assistant District Attorney Joseph Barba. He worked specifically with the Fire Investigation Division and he was the prosecutor who would handle the cases once they were cleared for court. We had worked together many times and spent many long nights putting the finishing touches on a case before court the next day. He was a good man and he wasn't afraid to go after the cases that were questionable. He gave each case his all and he made sure he put every ounce of strength and energy into getting guilty verdicts.

"ADA Barba," he said, as he picked up the call.

"Barba, it's Cole. I need a warrant for security footage and a customer transaction list for Spy Guy. Store owner's name is Seth Rogers."

"Probable cause?"

"A fire this morning at 467 Wilton Street killed thirty-seven year old Shelby Lewis and her two kids, a ten year old boy and an eight year old girl. Cameras were discovered all around the house. I took one of them back to the crime lab. Hank was able to get a serial number off of it and connect it back to the inventory that Mr. Rogers received. Unfortunately, Rogers is requesting a warrant before handing anything over to protect his customer's privacy. He deals with a lot of private detectives and wannabe spies."

"I'll start working on the warrant, you should have it within a few hours. Who do you want me to call when it's in?"

I could issue a warrant and do a

seizure of the evidence. The trick was more and more recently in court defense attorneys were questioning the chain of custody. As a fire investigator, I could not arrest anyone and had no formal clearance to obtain evidence. I could examine evidence as it pertained to my case, but I couldn't be the one to physically collect it. At least not without risking the case in court, which I wasn't about to do. It was a small annoyance, because it meant there had to be someone else, someone in law enforcement, who would have to collect the evidence and record it before I would be able to get my hands on it. It was an extra step and I really didn't like having a middleman, but I couldn't risk it. Not with this case.

"Detective Jonah West. He can serve

the warrant and collect the evidence. He is already been briefed on the case and running the victim."

"I'll send it his way once it's in. Anything else?"

"No, that's it. Thank you."

He ended the call and I tossed my phone back onto the seat with a sigh. I had nothing that I could do right now. I was stuck waiting on warrants and evidence. I knew the only thing I could do at that point was to go back to my place and start going over the new crime scene. Maybe something would be different with this one compared to the others and it would give me a new lead that I could chase down. I also didn't know when Hawke would be showing up and I didn't want to not be there when he arrived. With nothing left to do, I turned my car back on and started to make the drive back to my apartment.

CHAPTER TEN

Hawke

IT WAS A few hours later when I made my way back up to Tristan's apartment. It still bothered me that he lived in an apartment like this. He was too nice and not the kind of a man to live in a dump like this place. I really hoped that once this case was closed and he was able to get justice for himself and his parents that he would see he could have something better in his life.

That he was worth something more.

I had no doubt that he had feelings of low self-worth. The way his grandparents handled raising him after his parents' death was not what a traumatized child needed and it clearly had a lasting impact on Tristan. Hopefully, closure would be enough to give Tristan a new outlook on life and bring him some peace.

I knocked on his door and waited for him to open the door. I had sent him a text letting him know that I was on my way. I wanted to make sure he was home before I just showed up.

The door opened a few moments later and I could see that Tristan was exhausted. He looked tired yesterday, but the dark bags under his eyes were getting darker. I had noticed earlier that he appeared worn-out, but I figured it had to do with going to bed late and being woken up early. Hell, I was weary, too, and I had chugged a cup of coffee on my way over to the new crime scene. I had bounced back though, and it appeared that Tristan had only grown more drained as the hours ticked by. He moved back so I could walk in as he spoke.

"I appreciate you coming back. I know you are tired and probably want to be home on your day off."

"Don't worry about it. I normally just sit on my couch and tell myself I should clean as I binge hawatch all of the shows that I've missed all week."

"Do you ever clean?" he asked,

flashing a small smile.

"When I run out of dishes. And that is one hell of an accomplishment, believe me, because most of my dishes are paper or throw away pans," I said, with a smirk turning up the corners of my lips.

I had no problem with cooking or doing basic chores, but there was just something about dishes that I couldn't stand. It's why I had a dishwasher and a healthy supply of throw away dishes. I only wished frying pans or pots could be throw away as well.

"Wow, that is an accomplishment."

"What about you?" I asked as we went and plopped down on the couch.

"I like doing dishes. I like the peace and the repetitive motion to it. It helps me think, or not think, depending on what I need."

"I get that," I said gently, before I switched to a more joking tone to try and put a smile back on his face. "You know, if you ever run out of dishes to wash, I can pretty much guarantee you that my sink will have a bunch that you are welcome to indulge yourself in."

Tristan gave a huff of a laugh before he spoke. "Deal, but you have to do my laundry."

"You don't like laundry? That's the best adult chore. You just stick it in and forget about it. It practically does itself."

"Until you have to fold it or hang it up. Or worse, iron something."

"Ooooh, yeah I see your point on that one. I don't have to iron anything unless I have to wear my dress uniform, which is thankfully, almost never. And I almost never hang anything up. I just shove it in a drawer.”

“Your life skills are impressive,” he teased.

“They really are. You should see me in a grocery store. I can get in and out within fifteen minutes,” I said, flashing him a big smile as he chuckled slightly.

“It’s official, you have mastered adulting better than me.”

“I’ll give you some pointers,” I said with a playful wink before I moved the conversation back on topic. “So, I went back and searched through a lot of fires that were mostly deemed nuisance fires, but nothing really popped. I spoke to some old timers, and they didn’t remember any fires that appeared to be practice runs. But, a retired captain, Captain Atwater, he remembered three cases where they found close to a dozen cameras all over the house and one was even an apartment."

"An apartment?" he asked, confused and surprised,

I had also been shocked, because up until now our guy had always hit a house. Most arsonists did homes or warehouses just because they were easier. Going after an apartment in a building had a lot of risk and they couldn't control the fire as well. As much as it contradicts logic, arsonists liked control. They liked to be in command of the fire and watch as it ate everything in its path.

"Fifty-eight apartments, a hundred and thirty occupants with a mixture of adults and children. It was twenty-five years ago. I went and pulled the file, it was classified as an electrical malfunction and the owner was charged with various negligent charges, and received five years probation. The apartment building itself was made out of cement, but the apartments were wood, so it went up pretty quick. Sixty-five people were injured from smoke inhalation, minor burns, second degree and third degree burns, and broken bones from being pushed or stepped on. And by some miracle, no deaths. Multiple fire houses combed through the building and Captain Atwater remembered one of the apartments where the fire originated from having these small cameras all over the place. He assumed they were security cameras or some kinky sex thing."

"He's never hit an apartment before. That could be his first real fire. Did they have any suspects, anyone they talked to?"

I could hear the excitement in his voice, not that I could blame him. This was the first time we were getting a better picture of the arsonist. There was a very real chance that the apartment building fire was his first attempt at arson and just like most serial criminals, they strike in their comfort zone first before branching out. When someone was a serial criminal, whether that is a killer, rapist, arsonist, thief, whoever, they always committed their first crimes in their comfort zone, meaning their neighborhood. They felt safe there, they knew the routines of their neighbors. They knew the back and side alleys, the escape routes. It was all familiar to them, making them feel safe enough to finally do the one thing they had been craving. Once they built their confidence up, they got smarter. They no longer shit where they eat, making it more difficult to trace them back to their area.

"Unfortunately, no. They assumed it was electrical. The fire originated in the electrical panel, but they couldn't pinpoint exactly whose it was by the time the fire had burned through the apartments. He didn't remember them ever mentioning someone of interest and he never looked at anyone. I tried to find the file, but it was in the thousands that had gotten destroyed ten years ago from a flood. Captain Atwater was pretty new to the job back then, and most people didn't listen to him, but he did say he always had a weird feeling about it. He had a hard time believing that it just went up by itself."

"Why the feeling?"

"He chalked it up to being a new guy and being suspicious of everything and everyone. But, he said the building owner never wavered in his claim of being innocent. The contractors and electricians who had a hand in building the apartment building, they all checked out. They were all licensed and they only hired licensed employees. They had been around for fifteen years with not a single complaint. Captain Atwater said it never seemed right to him that out of fifteen years of building homes and apartment buildings, that this one went up due to a mistake. It simply defied logic. They also passed multiple inspections along the way and everything was up to code. At the time though, no one was interested in looking deeper and took it at face value. There was a good number of injuries, but no one died."

It wasn't surprising that no one wanted to look too closely at a fire that didn't have casualties. Fires were hard enough to investigate, but when you talk about ones that large, it was a nightmare that could take months to comb through. Twenty-five years ago, there just weren't enough fire investigators to handle the full city. Back then, if it quacked like a duck, looked like a duck, then it was a duck and no one dared to make it into something else.

"We don't have a suspect, but we have an area now that we can cross reference when we have a list of suspects. Hank, the Digital Forensic

Expert at the Crime Lab, was able to tease out a serial number from the camera. It came back to an inventory at Spy Guy, a go-to spot for private detectives and wannabe spies. I went to see the owner, but he demanded a warrant. I have ADA Barba getting that and he will issue it to Detective West who will collect the security footage and customer list. Once he has it, he will send it my way. Hopefully, that will give us something."

Hurry up and wait, basically. We couldn't do much until we could get our hands on some more evidence. The security footage and customer list would be very helpful. We could cross-reference the customers with the address of the apartment fire. Until we had that evidence though, we were sitting around doing nothing. There wasn't anything we could do, which meant I should leave, but that was the last thing I wanted to do.

"I'm sure it will. You must be feeling excited to finally be close to cracking this case. You've been working on it for over a decade now."

"I don't think excited is the word I would use to describe how I'm feeling. This is as close to a real lead that I've had since I started, but I've had times where I thought something would give me a lead only for it to not work out. I learned a long time ago not to hope and just to wait for the results."

I could understand that, but it was also sad at the same time. Everyone deserved to have hope, even if it was just a small piece of it. I could understand why he didn't want to hope. He had been doing this for over ten years, and that would take a toll on anyone. It was only natural that he wouldn't want to allow himself to anticipate finally having some success, that he would want to keep himself guarded from the potential disappointment and hurt. This wasn't just a simple arsonist that he had been hunting down. This was the arsonist who had killed his parents and left him permanently scarred. There was a deep personal and psychological connection to catching this man. If he never caught him, he was never going to have closure. He was never going to be able to move on and finally heal from it. It would break him the rest of the way and that wasn't something I ever wanted to see.

"I can understand you not wanting to

open yourself up to potential hurt and disappointment. I know how important this case is for you. How important it is for you to find the man responsible for your parents' death. I'm going to do everything I can to help you get justice for them. You're not doing this alone anymore," I said warmly as I took the chance and placed my hand on his knee.

I had no idea how he would respond to physical touching. We hadn't touched outside of a handshake and that was through my work gloves. He didn't come across as someone who enjoyed his personal space being invaded, but I hoped this was okay.

I wasn't blind. I could see that he was attracted to me. I was attracted to him and I wasn't one for ignoring my own feelings. I didn't know if I wanted to jump into a relationship, not with it still being close to my last relationship. However, I was open to taking things slow and seeing where it went. We could start off with a light relationship and if it grew then great, but if it didn't there was no harm, no foul. It was completely up to him, though. I wasn't going to push. He had complete control and we could play at his speed.

Tristan turned more toward me as he spoke. "I really appreciate everything you have done to help me. I know this isn't your job and you have no obligation to help me. It means a lot that you've helped me and believed me about these cases."

"I'm happy to assist. You have good instincts and because of them, I have faith that you will solve a lot of cases and put this arsonist behind bars where he belongs. You could have taken the easy way out and ignored these cases. But you didn't. You're doing something very brave by facing the emotional pain connected to these cases to get them justice. That's not easy and most people wouldn't be willing to do it."

He might not think that what he was doing was brave, but it was. I didn't know many people who would be willing to put themselves through the level of hurt this had to cause to get justice for strangers, for his parents. He brought up the trauma every time he looked at one of these cases. That didn't allow a wound to heal over and it definitely wasn't easy to live that way. He shouldn't have to live that way. It was one of the main reasons why I was willing to help him. He had been going at it alone, forced to be strong all the time, it was about time he had someone else in his corner. Someone who he could count on, rely on to be there for him when he needed a breather. Someone that could be the strong one when he couldn't be, and I was happy that he'd chosen me.

"It's the right thing to do."

To him, it truly was that simple. He was remarkable. He had every reason to hate the world, to want to ignore everything wrong in it and live his own life. And yet, he was working to try and give justice to people, to help put dangerous people behind bars. He was reliving his own childhood trauma to help others and he had no idea how remarkable he truly was. He had no idea how special and amazing that made him.

"You're amazing, Darlin'. I just wish you could see it for yourself."

There was a flash of emotion that went through his eyes, but I wasn't able to pinpoint exactly what emotion it was. I suspected it was a mixture of surprise, confusion, and self-loathing, but I couldn't be certain. I hated that he didn't see how special he was. I hated that his grandparents, people who were supposed to love him and lift him up, had ignored him and torn him down. I was sure they hadn't realized the repercussions their actions would have on him. I was sure they were grieving at the time and having to bury a child was never easy, no matter the age. I understood all of that, but while they were wrapped up in their own grief, they allowed their grandson to be mentally and emotionally neglected. Something that was going to take a long time to repair in him.

Tristan slowly leaned in toward me and I was instantly surprised by the action. I knew what he was going for, but I didn't expect it. It was clear that we were both attracted to each other. It was easy to tell with the way his gaze was constantly traveling down to my lips. I couldn't tell you how badly I wanted to grab him and kiss him, but I was afraid he wouldn't react well to that.

I didn't pull back and I didn't really move in. I was afraid that if I moved in to meet his lips that he would pull back. That he would be snapped out of the moment and I would miss my chance to taste him.

When our lips finally touched, a jolt of electricity shot through my whole body. I instantly pressed my lips harder against his. I wanted to make sure that Tristan knew I wanted this just as badly as he did. I moved my hand over and placed it on the bottom of his jawline on his right side, deepening the kiss as I licked at his lips, seeking entrance.

Tristan gave a soft moan like he was all too happy to open his mouth and allow our tongues to dance together. He tasted amazing and he was no longer shy. The uncertainty he had when the kiss started was long gone and Tristan was not afraid to go after what he wanted. I loved the confidence he now had.

The soft purring moans slipping from his throat were driving me insane. I was already hard and I suspected he was as well. The sexual desire that sparked between us was consuming the both of us and I knew neither one of us wanted it to stop.

All too soon, I had to pull back so we could catch our breaths. I didn't pull back very far though. We stayed close and I lightly pressed my forehead against his.

"Wow," Tristan whispered on a breath.

"I know. We should probably stop." I said the words, but I really didn't want to say them. I wanted to give him an out, though. I wanted to give him the chance to pump the brakes if he needed it. I really hoped he didn't need it, though. Stopping was the very last thing I wanted right now.

"Do you want to stop?" he asked, and I could hear that he was worried about me regretting this. Regret was not an emotion I experienced right now. It was the furthest thing from what I felt.

"Fuck no," I answered, honestly.

"Good."

Tristan placed his hand on the back of my neck and pulled me back in for another kiss. All of the control was gone now on both of our ends. Now that we had established what we both wanted, there was no stopping us.

Tristan pulled me down so he was lying on the couch and I happily fitted myself between legs that he willingly opened to accommodate me. Our new position only fueled our need as our dicks pressed against each other. Tristan moved his hands down my back and over to my jean-clad ass and pressed me down against him, forcing more contact between our dicks.

I ground my hips against his and we both let out a deep moan as we rubbed against each other. I knew it had been about two months since the last time I had sex, but based on how hungry Tristan was, I was willing to bet it had been much longer for him.

His hips met mine as we both ground and thrust against one another. I needed to feel more of him, though. There wasn't nearly enough contact with him through our clothes. Before I even had a chance to pull back, Tristan spoke.

"I need to feel you inside of me."

That one sentence sent electricity racing through every nerve in my body and it landed straight in my groin. For the rest of my life, I would never hear a sentence sexier than those few words sounded coming from his kiss-swollen lips. I placed my hand on the back of his neck and pulled him up as I spoke.

"Bedroom."

I pressed my lips against his as Tristan guided us down the hallway to his bedroom. We continued to kiss, only pulling apart long enough for us to remove the other's shirt before our mouths were back on each other. Thankfully, the trip to his bedroom was very short and by the time we reached it we were both fumbling on the other's belt and pants. The very second that I could, I shoved my down his boxers and I finally got to feel his hot, engorged dick against my hand.

Tristan let out a long, drawn out

moan at the contact of finally having skin on skin and he quickly followed my lead and then it was my turn to let out a deep gravely moan as he wrapped his fist tightly around my already throbbing cock.

There was no way I was going to be able to control myself with him. He felt too good and the needy moans he was making were killing me. I was trying to control myself. I was trying to take it slow, but I felt like my whole body was going to burst into flames.

I walked him back toward the bed, both of us stepping out of our pants and boxers as we moved. Tristan fell onto the bed and backed up until he was lying on his pillows and I followed. I had no choice but to break the kiss so I could speak.

"You got stuff?"

"Top drawer," he said as he pointed to his bedside table.

I quickly reached over and pulled out the bottle of lube and a condom before I turned my attention back to the delicious looking body waiting for me. He looked so good. He was thin, but he had some muscle definition. Nothing crazy, but I could tell he tried to stay in shape. I suspected he was a runner based on his leg muscles. I saw a flicker of self-consciousness as he moved his left arm up toward his pillow to try and hide it. As if he thought if I saw his burn that would ruin everything.

I wasn't about to let him get away with that.

I reached over and took his left hand in mine and turned it so I could see his arm. Before he even had a chance to say anything, I pressed my lips to the back of his hand and kissed my way all the way up his arm, across his shoulder, and up his neck, before I lightly bit on his earlobe and spoke as I started to travel down his chest.

"Don't ever feel like you have to hide from me. You're beautiful, every single inch of you."

Tristan let out a soft moan as I kissed my way down his chest and over his stomach until I reached his glorious dick nestled in a thatch of dark curls. The slit was already dripping with precum and I knew it wouldn't be long before he was coming in my mouth. My mouth watered at just the thought of what Tristan tasted like. I looked up at him as I ran my tongue along his shaft, pausing just before the dripping head of his cock, causing his breath to hitch as he watched me.

"Oh God, just when I thought you couldn't get any sexier," he said, as he locked his eyes on mine.

I smirked before I took his tip into my mouth and sucked on it, causing him to let out a hiss. I moaned my appreciation as his unique flavor burst over my tongue and I finally got to taste him. Just as I'd suspected, he was the perfect blend of sweet and salty.

I wanted more.

I *needed* more.

I took him all the way down to his base and I couldn't help but let a grumbly moan tumble from my throat as I felt his hardness slide over my tongue. I felt Tristan run his hand into my hair and I could tell by how tense his hand was he was doing everything he could to keep himself from thrusting into my mouth.

I continued to work his cock as I flicked open the lid of the tube of lube. Slathering the slick liquid on three of my fingers, I moved my hand to pluck gently at his puckered hole. He relaxed and pressed back against my hand with his unspoken request, and I gradually inserted my index finger bit by bit into his tight ass. I didn't know how long it had been since he had last been stretched and I didn't want to just jump right in with two fingers. I was glad for my control and the presence of mind to be vigilant and careful with him as he gripped around my finger. I paused for a moment to allow him to get used to the intrusion. The last thing I wanted to do was hurt him or cause him any pain.

When his muscles relented, allowing me movement once more, I slowly worked my finger in and out of him, keeping my mouth wrapped around his pulsing shaft. He was still so very tight but with the combined pleasure of my mouth and fingers, he started to loosen up until he was back to moaning and whimpering for more.

Once I felt like he was ready, I added a second finger and began to truly stretch him out. I was relieved when Tristan started to wiggle his hips to get more of my fingers inside of him. He was starting to really loosen up and become comfortable with me. I added a third finger and began to look for his sweet spot, that one place that would make him scream. The second my fingers ran over it, Tristan gave a loud moan as he thrust his hips up, pushing his dick even deeper into my mouth. I moaned at the sensation of his dick pushing further into my mouth and I continued to rub circles over his sweet spot.

"Oh fuck, you're gonna make me come," he warned, but I had no interest in pulling my mouth off. I had to taste him and I was not going to stop until I got it.

It was only a moment later when Tristan's hips snapped up and he gave a hoarse cry as he came hot and hard down my throat. I moaned as his sweet taste flooded my mouth. I easily swallowed what Tristan had to give me as he continued to twitch.

Once he stopped pulsing, I removed

my fingers from his hole and pulled my mouth off of his dick. Tristan instantly pulled me in for a passionate kiss. Our tongues danced with each other and he moaned as the taste of his essence flooded his own mouth.

I reached over for the condom and easily slid it on as our tongues continued to dance with each other. I felt Tristan opening his legs up wider for me as I lowered myself between his legs. I pulled back from the kiss and moved my hand down to my dick as I lined up to his hole. Tristan angled his hips up and I placed my hands on the back of his thighs to lift his hips up more. I placed my tip against his pucker and slowly pushed in.

I wanted to pound the hell out of him, but I knew I had to go slow at first. Even though I had stretched him, he was still so very tight and I didn't want to hurt him. Slowly, I moved inch by inch, watching as my dick disappeared inside of him until I was buried balls deep. Tristan wrapped his legs around my hips and I placed my forehead against his as we both tried to catch our breaths.

"Holy shit, you feel fucking amazing," I whispered as I fought not to move.

"So do you. So big, so fucking big. I'm good, move," Tristan said with need dripping from his voice.

I didn't need to be told twice, not when it felt this good. I pulled out almost all of the way before I pressed back in, causing us both to moan. I went slow at first, but once I felt him truly starting to adjust to my size, I didn't need to hold back.

"So good, Baby. So tight."

Tristan's hands went to my back and his nails dug into my skin as I snapped my hips hard and fast, pushing all of my dick deep inside of him. Tristan angled his hips once again, and I started to look for his sweet spot. I knew I hit it dead on when he let out a scream of pleasure.

"Fuck yes," Tristan moaned through panted breaths.

I moved my hand over to Tristan's dick and I started to jerk him off in time with my thrusts. Both of us were a writhing moaning mess. Neither one of us could seem to get enough of each other. I never wanted this to end. Being inside of him, it felt like we had done this a million times. He was home to me and I never wanted to be anywhere else.

"I'm so close," he mewled, his fingers

gripping my biceps so hard I was sure to have bruises tomorrow. I didn't care. I loved it.

"Me too. I want to feel you come. Come for me, Darlin'," I ordered as I picked up my pace.

I could feel his legs shaking from the pleasure coursing through him. After a few more thrusts, Tristan let out loud, keening cry.

"Hawke," he called out as he came hard once again, jet after jet of jizz escaping his slit as his dick twitched and pulsed in my fist.

The tightening of his walls around my dick was enough to push me over the edge. Electricity raced up my spine and I snapped my hips forward, going as deep as I let myself go.

"Tris!" I groaned as I erupted inside of

him.

Tristan's legs fell from my hips and he collapsed back against the pillows, boneless and with a half-lidded, sated look crossing his features. I dropped down over him before I leaned in to press my mouth against his. We were both out of breath, but neither of us were ready to lose the physical connection to the other.

I brought my hand up to the side of his face as we continued to slowly kiss, our tongues tangling once more. I knew I would have to let him go eventually, we were both going to need some serious sleep after this, but for right now, I was more than happy to simply kiss him and hold him as our bodies calmed back down.

CHAPTER ELEVEN

Tristan

AS QUIETLY AS I could, I climbed out of my bed and grabbed some sweatpants and a t-shirt before I made my way out of my bedroom and back to the living room. The glowing clock on my stove told me it was just after two in the morning. I had only slept maybe an hour, assuming I was that lucky.

I was used to not being able to sleep. I was used to having my mind racing with different thoughts. Tonight they weren't racing because of past memories or a case, though. Tonight, I couldn't get my mind to turn off because I was mentally freaking out about having sex with Hawke.

This was all kinds of bad.

We were working together. We would still see each other even after this case was closed. I'd never slept with anyone who was connected to my job, because I didn't want that awkwardness at work. I shouldn't have done it. I can normally keep myself in line and yet, for some reason with Hawke, I couldn't resist him.

Once again when he'd touched me it felt like a fire had exploded within my body. And once again he felt familiar. I had never been with him. I hadn't met him before this and yet, my whole body was reacting to him like I had known him my whole life. It was ridiculous and made zero sense. No matter how much I try to ignore it, my body didn't want to listen.

I had to put distance back between us. I had to get my mind focused again. I couldn't let Hawke's presence distract me. I couldn't let him break down all of my walls. Last night was a slip up and it wasn't one I could allow to happen again.

Letting out a sigh, I plopped down on my couch. I glanced at my phone and noticed that Detective West had sent me the evidence that he'd collected from Spy Guy.

I opened my laptop up and pulled up

Detective West's email. I had to focus on what truly mattered—catching my parents' killer. I couldn't afford to let Hawke distract me again. Too much was riding on me finding this arsonist. Too many victims were counting on me to solve their case and get them justice. I couldn't let a pretty face distract me any longer. Even if he made me feel things I had never felt before.

***

It was nearing four in the morning when I heard footsteps coming toward the living room. I looked over and saw Hawke standing there in just his jeans as he leaned against the doorjamb into the living room. It took all of my strength to keep my gaze on his and not to let my eyes wander down over his very toned chest and stomach. The man was ridiculously sexy. He was sexy to the point where it just wasn't fair.

The man was all muscle, including a delicious six pack that made my mouth water. There wasn't an ounce of fat on him and don't even get me started on his strong thighs and amazing looking ass. He was sex on a stick and it was not fair. Not because I couldn't sleep with him again, but because there was nothing I could do in a gym that would ever make me look as good as him.

I didn't even have a one pack.

I wasn't chubby or out of shape, but I was flat. I didn't work out. I hated the gym. It was why I always ran outside. Running was the only form of exercise that I enjoyed doing, to an extent, and it didn't give me tight-as-sin abs. I had some muscles on my arms from just typically lifting at crime scenes, and my legs were in good shape, but I was nothing compared to him.

I couldn't stop the flood of images that invaded my mind as I tried to not oogle him. My mind apparently had other ideas, though, because all I could see was our time together just a few short hours ago. The pleasure that he'd brought to my body was unlike anything I had ever felt before. Sex had always felt okay to me, but it was never something that my body craved, at least until Hawke showed up in my life.

We'd only gone one round last night, but I could have gone for another six and still wanted more. I wasn't used to that. I wasn't used to craving someone.

To being horny.

HAWKE

I knew it was stupid, because I had been a typical hormonal teenager, but even then I had never been too interested in sex. I always figured that was just my personality. Not everyone was interested in sex. Not everyone spent their time in the shower masturbating. Plus, I had a lot going on with the fire and adjusting to life without my parents at that point. It was only logical for sexual activity to take a backseat.

Now it felt like this monster inside of me had woken up after being in hibernation for fifteen years and it was starving. As if there was no amount of food that I could feed it for it to finally be happy and satisfied. Even sitting there, I had to fight with my growing erection. Just the sight of the man was enough to make me want to get down on my knees or bend over for him.

I felt like a bitch in heat.

It was pathetic and I was above that behavior. Now I just needed my dick to understand it.

"Sorry, did I wake you?" I asked.

"No, I rolled over and you weren't there. You've been looking more tired each day, and I figured you were having a hard time sleeping. Now I've confirmed that theory. Do you want to talk about it?"

Talking about my screwed up mind was not something I wanted to do.

Not now. Not ever.

Thankfully, I had something that would work beautifully to change the topic without coming across as emotionally damaged.

"Detective West sent me the customer list and security footage from Spy Guy. I've just been combing through it."

"I'll make some coffee," he said, flashing me a warm smile as he strolled over to the kitchen. The fact that he already knew where my coffee was kept should have bothered me and yet, it felt right somehow. Something else I chose to ignore. I was getting very good at ignoring what was happening between us. At least, my emotions about it.

"Anyone pop?" he asked as he got the coffee maker going.

"Not yet. There's audio, but so far it's a bunch of guys who think they are all James Bond. I've been going through the customer list, but it's only debit and credit cards. He doesn't keep track of cash transactions, so we might not get him that way. I'm hoping we can get him on camera. Spy Guy has a website, but you can't order online so he'd have had to go in to get the cameras."

"And we're sure it's not the owner?"

"Everything about him is clean. Detective West looked into him, but he doesn't think he's our guy. He also has an alibi for the Rollins' fire. He was out of town. Credit card transactions put him two hundred miles away at some spy conference. He didn't get back until yesterday morning."

"He's definitely out, then. It would also be stupid for him to use cameras from his own inventory since they could easily be traced back to him. My guess is it's a new customer. If our guy knew about these cameras before, he would have made the switch even if he had some of the old ones left." He brought over two mugs of hot coffee, handing me one. He even knew how I took it.

How could it be possible for someone to know me so well after such a short amount of time?

We'd barely even spoken about anything personal and yet, he had paid enough attention to notice what I put in my coffee, just like I knew what he put in his.

He sat down next to me and I could feel the heat from his body. It was doing nothing to calm my own body, or my desire to reach out and feel him. It would be so simple, too. I could run my fingers over his leg, down his back. Hell, I could straddle his lap and I got the impression he would be all for it. I had to force my mind to inform my body to not move. It should have been simple, but I felt like my body was fighting me. As if I was drowning and it was taking everything I had to not breathe in the water. It shouldn't be this hard, and yet, it was.

"You know, normally I have a feeling about cases. I can get a rough idea of who the arsonist is. The places he picks, the people he targets, how he does it, if he leaves people alive or kills them. Are the targets empty or have people in them. I can get a profile and a picture of him in my mind. This time, though, I can't *see* him. I don't know if it's because he's smarter than me or because I can't get past the emotional part of the case this time around," I admitted as the security footage continued to play in the background for us to watch.

"He's not smarter than you. Yes, you are emotionally connected to the investigation, but sometimes I think that can be a good thing. If you weren't emotionally connected, would you still be investigating these cases? Would you have suspected it was an arsonist? Would you have connected the cameras? Sometimes, being emotionally involved can lead to disaster, but then there are times when that connection is everything to the case. All of those people will have a chance at getting justice because of your connection. I don't see that as a disadvantage, Darlin'."

And just like that I felt better.

What the hell was it about him that made the voices in my head go quiet?

My grandparents were never mean to me. They never raised their hand to me.

They never belittled me or put me down. They weren't terrible people, they were just absent mentally and emotionally. And yet, I couldn't help but feel like I wasn't good enough. Whenever I couldn't solve a case in a reasonable amount of time, I felt like I was failing, like I wasn't good enough. I wasn't smart enough, quick enough, to stop the arsonist before his next fire. I had never been able to silence the voices but a few words from Hawke and they were gone.

I didn't understand any of it. I shouldn't feel connected to him. I shouldn't feel this relaxed around him. I definitely shouldn't be talking about my past or my feelings. I swore to myself I wouldn't. I swore that I would keep the walls up and be nothing but professional with him, but there we were. I had gone against my own promise to myself and fallen for his beautiful eyes.

The sex had been epic, and I couldn't say I regretted it. I should, though. I should be kicking myself for ever even allowing it to happen. I couldn't, though, because it had been the best night of my life. It was a sad fact, because at my age having a one-night stand shouldn't qualify as my best of anything, but it was.

It was better in person than it had been in any of the dreams that still haunted me. I needed to keep my distance from him, but I didn't want to and that didn't scare me as nearly as much as it should have.

"Look, about last night," I started, but Hawke cut me off.

"You don't have to say anything," He

started, but it was my turn to cut him off. I had no idea what he was going to say. I was honestly too afraid to hear it, because if he said it was a mistake I was going to lose every ounce of courage I had managed to scrounge up.

"I don't regret it. In truth, it was the best night I've ever had. I'm not good with social situations. I used to be, but after the fire my world got so much smaller and now I don't know how to make it grow. What I do know is that I like being around you. I'm really terrible at this, though. I don't do relationships, mostly because that would mean I'd have to be vulnerable and I'm really not good at that part." I let out a soft sigh before I continued. "Look, what I'm trying to say is, I don't see last night as a mistake. I understand if you do."

"I don't. I don't regret a single second of last night. I don't see it as a mistake. I was worried you might see it that way and I couldn't handle hearing you say it. I can't tell you how happy I am to hear you say it wasn't a mistake. And for the record, I am terrible at relationships, too. I just got out of one not too long ago. We dated for two years and the whole time he was in the closet. I kept telling myself that he wasn't lying about coming out, that the excuses he made were justified. It took two years of being a dirty secret before I'd finally had enough and left. So, I'm not really good at this either, but I'm willing to learn with you."

My heart started to flutter in my chest at his words. This was stupid, I shouldn't be reacting this way to him, but I couldn't help it. Just hearing that he didn't see last night as a mistake, that he wanted to potentially see where this could go, it made me feel excited, hopeful, and those were two emotions I hadn't felt in many years.

"I'd really like that," I said, flashing him a warm smile.

God, what the hell was it about this man?

He gave me a sexy smile as he turned and started to close the gap between us. I didn't even hesitate to move in and the second his lips touched mine, I let out a soft moan. I had never really liked kissing, but the way he did it, the way his lips felt against mine, I was quickly becoming addicted to it.

All too soon, though, he was snapping back and looking at the computer as he spoke.

"I know that voice."

I looked over at the computer to see who was speaking. I didn't recognize the voice softly playing in the background or the image. They weren't talking about anything really, the man was just asking Mr. Rogers for his order. Apparently, he had called it in.

"Who is he?"

"That's Taye Amaro. He's a firefighter at Station House Seventeen."

"Amaro? My Captain is Damon Amaro, are they related?"

"Taye is Damon's older brother."

Holy shit.

There was no reason for Taye to be buying anything from Spy Guy. His name also wasn't on the transaction list, so he obviously paid in cash.

It would also explain why my Captain

didn't want me to look into any of these cases. Why he was happy to let them be closed to accidental or go into the cold case box. Taye would know how to start a fire with being a firefighter, he also would have access to test houses. He could have started a fire for them to run drills and no one would be the wiser of it.

"That's the camera." I said, as a medium size box was placed on the counter and Taye pulled one of the small packages out of it.

"Based on the package size, there's got to be easily a hundred cameras inside that box. We only found ten. How far back is this?"

"A week. I started at the most recent and was working my way back. If he is buying that many, my guess is that means he'd already bought some before to test it out. He could be testing them at the firehouse in the burn house. I don't know anything about him. Have you worked with him?"

There were plenty of firefighters that I had never worked with nor seen before. I only went to places where arson was suspected. If they didn't suspect any foul play, then there was no need to have a fire investigator there. With Hawke being a firefighter, he was more likely to have worked with Taye or seen him at the fire bar—a bar that catered only to first responders.

"I haven't worked with him, but I've seen him at the bar. We've talked a few times, but I don't tend to stay around him long. People tend to give him a wide berth when they can. He's a bit... fuck, I don't even know. He's got anger issues, and he has an issue with authority. That's why he's only a Lieutenant even though he's forty. He's odd, and when I've been around him I get a bad vibe from him. He has some friends, guys who are a lot like him and others who respect him because he's a legacy. Both him and his brother are firefighters, obviously, but so was his father, his grandfather, and his great grandfather. All of them joined the Fire Department at eighteen and were Captain or higher ranking. Taye is the black sheep."

"It would make sense if he was an arsonist. They tend to be socially odd. They don't like authority and can have anger issues. Being around fire, it would have helped to ease his compulsion and obsession with it. He's forty, so he would have been fifteen with the apartment fire."

"Is that possible? It seems like he would have been too young to be able to get away with a fire like that."

It was too young.

Not too young to set a house on fire, but it was too young to take on an apartment building like that. Someone would have noticed him. He wouldn't have been able to build the device and get away with it. He wouldn't have known about putting cameras up. It was why I believed so strongly that it was two people.

A mentor and mentee.

It was looking like Taye was the mentee and now we needed to find the mentor, assuming he was even still alive.

"He would have been. Even if he lived

there, it would have been too complicated for him to pull off by himself, especially with it coming back as accidental. My gut is telling me that he's the apprentice; we need the master for older fires. Do you know of any stressors in his life? Something that may have made him snap?"

"I don't know him that well. I know ten years ago his father died in a fire on the job. Apparently it was a really bad fire. His father, Henry, was a Station Chief with House Forty-Two. They were called to a storage facility fire. It was supposed to be simple enough, but the place was filled with smoke and his men kept getting turned around. One of the storage units was storing propane and it all went up. The Chief went in and he never came back out, along with two of his men."

"That would be enough to push his desire for fires into overdrive. You don't just walk up to someone, though, and ask them to teach you how to get away with arson. He must have found his teacher somehow, maybe someone who was close to him already and had seen the signs."

"He's a firefighter though, why would he need a mentor to begin with? It's not like he wouldn't know how to start a fire or how to control one. He doesn't seem to have the personality type to be submissive either."

"Which would mean that the original arsonist approached him. He had to have been in Taye's life to know that Taye would be interested in starting fires. He's gotta be in his personal circle."

The trick was going to be finding that person. Neither one of us knew Taye, really, so if we started asking people at his fire house about him, it would start to raise red flags and questions would be asked. We could spook him and lose him forever or worse, force his hand to do something incredibly dangerous and put even more people at risk.

"We can't ask any of his friends or him without tipping him off. How good of a man is your Captain?"

I let out a deep breath before I spoke.

"I don't know. I mean, he's always willing to help with a case. He wants our cases to be closed and to get to the truth. I've never had a problem with him. At the same time though, he didn't want me looking into these cases. He doesn't believe they are connected. I thought maybe he was against it because he truly believed I was seeing shit, but now, I don't know. Maybe he suspected it was his brother and he's been trying to cover it up."

"He is the only one out of his family so far to not be a physical firefighter. He's like you, he went straight into investigations right from the academy. Maybe that was by design so he could cover up the fires connected to Taye or this mentor."

I wasn't liking any of this. None of this was playing out well in my mind. Either my Captain was involved and he knew what his older brother was doing and covering up his crimes, or he didn't know and I was going to have to fight him tooth and nail with evidence that his brother was an arsonist who was responsible for multiple deaths.

On top of all of that, they were legacies. That came with a level of respect that most people didn't receive. Taye being arrested for arson could destroy that legacy. When people heard the name Amaro, they wouldn't think about all of the good the family had done. It would be all about the fires and the people Taye had killed.

"Either way, I have to talk to my Captain. I have to see where he stands. It's the only play we have. Taye has easily a hundred more cameras. That's ten more fires, ten more chances of someone being killed. We don't have time to play this one close to the chest or slow walk it."

"Do you want me to go with you?"

"No, it's better for me to do this one-on-one. Thanks, though," I said, flashing him a warm smile at the offer.

"I have a shift in a couple of hours. I can ask the guys at the house if they know Taye. They've been around longer than me, they might have worked with him."

"Be careful, we don't know who could be close friends with him."

"Always. Why don't I make us some breakfast and we can keep going over the footage. Maybe there was someone else that bought a bulk order of the cameras," he offered.

I gave him a nod of acknowledgment, and he headed back into my kitchen. I knew I wouldn't find another customer who was buying the cameras in bulk, but it was something I had to do to ensure I could prove without a doubt that Taye was the only one to purchase the cameras.

I knew my Captain wasn't going to be happy about any of it. He wasn't going to want to admit to what was right in front of his face, not that I could blame him. Taye was his older brother; he wouldn't want to think that he could be responsible for someone like this. He was going to be hard to convince, but I had no choice but to convince him. Too much was riding on the line with this case. I just hoped I could get my Captain to see what I saw. If I couldn't, I didn't know what I would do.

CHAPTER TWELVE

Hawke

I HEADED INTO the Station House and made my way straight to the main area where the kitchen and living room was. The house was pretty cozy considering thirty guys all lived in it in opposite shifts. We tried to get along with the guys on the previous shift. Not moving things around when we know it drove one of the other guys crazy. We made sure to only eat the food in our fridge and not their fridge. We tried to keep it as civil and peaceful as we could.

It might sound silly to have to have two fridges or to keep the living room in the same position, but when you are trying to keep things civil with thirty people in one house, those things help to prevent war.

For the most part, it was all men there. We'd had a couple female paramedics, but they were floaters and typically only filled in until we could find a permanent replacement. Paramedics came and went a good chunk of the time. Last year we had twenty of them in one year. There was even one shift where I started the day and it was one guy, but by the end of my shift it was another one. Sometimes it was a revolving door around there.

I walked into the kitchen area and saw Zander cleaning up some dishes. I could see that the dishes annoyed him and I knew that meant they weren't his dishes he was washing. So either it was one of the guys on our shift who'd dumped them and run, or the guys from the other shift hadn't done their dishes. A huge pet peeve that Zander had. I couldn't blame him. We were all supposed to be responsible for our own cleanup.

"Who are we killing?" I asked with a smirk as I slid onto one of the bar stools at the counter.

"They're pigs. I get it, the shift was busy and they didn't have time in between calls to eat and clean up. But then one of them could at least stay and do their fucking dishes. We're not their maids and if any of us pulled this shit, they would be leaving them in our bunks," Zander snapped and I knew the frustration had been building for a while.

Things between the two shifts did come up and unfortunately, as humans we had personalities and those personalities didn't always play well with each other. There had even been a few times where I'd seen Cap going toe to toe with the other shift's Captain.

"I know, and I agree with you. I can send Sinclair a text letting him know that we don't appreciate the mess and to make sure it's cleaned up next time. In a very polite and non-confrontational tone," I offered, flashing him a warm smile.

I didn't care about confrontation, but often I was the one who had to play peacekeeper with the guys. Get a bunch of alpha males together and trap them in a house, and it didn't always end well. Every house needed guys like me who could play mediator and try to keep the alphas from tearing each other apart.

"You can let him know that the next time they want to leave their dirty fucking dishes everywhere, I'm putting itching powder in their bunks," he seethed.

"So many swear words and the shift just started," I teased.

Zander was very friendly, when someone didn't piss him off. He did swear though. Like, a lot. Sailors would be proud; some would even be offended by the words that had come out of his mouth. He was rough around the edges and when I first started there I was a bit worried about him. He was the definition of an alpha male. He was also a ladies man and I was worried he would have an issue with me being gay. He didn't care, though. We'd even had conversations about my sex life. It took a special man to be straight and not even bat an eye at sex talk with a gay man.

"Fuck off," he said, chuckling.

I gave a snigger. I decided to ask him about Taye before the others came in, or before that bell went off and we had to leave. "You are a frequent flier at the fire bar," I started, but he cut me off.

"Seems like there's an insult in that."

"There's not, just an observation." He didn't need me to tell him he was a manwhore. He already knew. In the time I had known him, he'd slept with close to a hundred different women. Sometimes multiple women in a single night.

"Mhm, and where is this observation going?" he asked, still dubious.

"Taye Amaro, you know anything about him?"

"He's not gay and if he is, he's so far deep in the closet he's living in Narnia. He's a homophobic asshole. Stay the hell away from him," he answered with an edge in his voice.

"I'm not interested in him like that. There's a chance he's connected to a series of fires. A friend of mine who is investigating the case asked if I knew him. I told him I would ask around the house with the guys. I know you frequent the same bar, though."

"That's not surprising. He hides it well, but I can see the darkness in his eyes. He's completely fake, but every now and then, when he thinks no one is looking, his mask slips and people see the devil that he is. If your friend thinks he's connected, then he probably is. Good luck finding anyone that truly knows him, though. He has a different face for each person he sees. He only shows fake interest with people who could get him somewhere or make him feel special."

"I've always gotten a bad vibe off of him. I've kept a distance between us and I don't tend to go to the fire bar very often. You ever hear any stories that he's told? Anything about a fire that maybe he was too interested in?"

I doubted he would be dumb enough

to talk about one of his own fires, but one never knew. He was arrogant enough to believe he would never get caught. Arsonists loved to relive their fires, it was why so many prefered to record it now. It allowed them to see it whenever they wanted and experience the thrill again without having to rely solely on their memory. Memories faded over time and they got spotty. They were easy to mix up if someone were trying to remember specifics, especially if they were responsible for multiple fires. Those little facts, little memories, they were what arsonists lived for, what they cherished. He would want to remember them, relive them, as often as he could in any form that he could.

"Nothing specific, really. He talks about fires on the job, always the ones that most of us never want to talk about. For him, it seemed like the more gruesome the better. The ones with horrible burn victims, alive and dead. He never talks about the accidents, the rescue calls. Even when the victims are mangled, he never cares about it. He only likes the fires and he has no problem spending hours talking about it. I don't know if this is true, but Keith from Thirty-Fifth, he did a fly by at House Nineteen when Taye was there. He swears that Taye had a scrapbook of some of the most horrific fires. He would look at them before going to sleep. Something is definitely off with that man."

Couldn't argue that. It all fit though, with who an arsonist was. If he did have a scrapbook, that could help Tristan with his case. It was quite possible that Taye had a scrapbook of the fires he started, little tokens to help him relive the fires when he wasn't able to watch the videos.

It was something that Tristan would be able to look into and hopefully find. That was assuming he would even be able to get Taye brought in alive. Most arsonists would go down in a blaze of glory, literally. They were not above setting themselves on fire to escape prison. They didn't care who else was killed in the process, and what scared me was that person very well could be Tristan.

"Thanks, I'll let him know. It's all preliminary right now. And obviously, he needs to be careful given that he's a firefighter and a legacy. I'd appreciate it if you didn't mention this to anyone."

"You don't even have to ask, Brother. Tell him to be careful, though. People don't like Taye and everyone might not be all that shocked by him starting fires, but that doesn't mean they will ignore the red wall. If he's going to go up against Taye, he better make sure there is no wiggle room with the evidence or someone could turn on him."

And that was my other fear. I was terrified that Taye was going to turn on Tristan and finish what his mentor had started. I was also terrified that the fire department was going to turn on Tristan after having Taye arrested.

Tristan didn't run into fires, so it wasn't like he had to worry about his fellow brothers leaving him in a fire. But he was still out in public. He went onto crime scenes and to the bar. They could go after him outside of work, where they wouldn't be followed or watched. It was extremely dangerous for him, and I was very worried about how easily all of it could blow back on him.

I knew it could also blow back on me, too, but I wasn't worried about myself. I knew my brothers at the house had my back, even if they might not agree with me. They would never let anything happen to me. I also knew they would believe the evidence and they'd know that I would never go after another firefighter unless I was one hundred percent certain he was in the wrong.

"He's being careful and he has a detective helping him with gathering evidence. He's not going to go after Taye unless he has solid evidence against him. He knows what's on the line."

"Good. Be smart."

The look he gave me told me everything I needed to know. He knew I had my hand in the proverbial cookie jar, but he wasn't going to try and convince me to take it out. He would support me through it no matter what, and that was one of the reasons why I loved him. He always had my back, whether I was right or wrong it didn't matter to him. If I was going to battle, he would be standing right next to me ready to go. Zander was a ride or die man and everyone needed a man like that in their life. I just hoped that we would both get through it unscathed.

I also hoped Tristan and I could get enough evidence to put Taye in prison and be able to start making a real go with whatever was going on between us. I was leaving the ball in his court and I really hoped he was going to serve it back to me. Only time would tell, and I had no choice but to wait and see what time had in store for the both of us.

We just had to get through the investigation first.

CHAPTER THIRTEEN

Tristan

I HAD MADE the walk to my Captain's office plenty of times in the past fifteen years, but I had never felt this nervous before at just the thought of seeing him. A Captain was supposed to be a firefighters' first line of defense. He was supposed to be the one person who would have their back and be there for them. He was supposed to help them and support them.

At least, that was what a Captain was supposed to be.

I had learned from other investigators and firefighters that it wasn't always the case. There were plenty of Captains and Chiefs who didn't have their team's back. Who didn't care to help. They sat in their office and did the work they had to do and ignored the work they didn't have to do. They didn't stick their necks out to fight for what was right. They didn't risk their careers by doing what was right. They were interested in doing what they had to do to get by and get their paycheck, and not a lick more.

Captain Amaro was a good man, we didn't have many issues between us. I knew he wasn't happy about me having these cases, but I didn't know why. At first, I figured it was because he didn't believe me. That he thought I was seeing something that wasn't there. Now, with this new information, it was very possible that he didn't want me looking into these cases because they were connected to his brother. I really hoped that wasn't the real reason.

I was taking a huge risk going to him right now. If he knew that his brother was starting these fires, he could tip him off. He could try and discredit me, ruin my career, just to keep these cases swept under the rug. I would have to fight all on my own.

Yes, Hawke was helping me, but there was only so much he could do. He wasn't an investigator. He was a firefighter. We played in the same world, but we were not playing the same sport.

There was no short supply of tension between the firefighters and the investigators. The firefighters tended to think investigators weren't real firefighters because they worked behind a desk and didn't go into a blazing inferno. They also assumed investigators were stuck up and that we thought we were better than them. Other investigators thought the firefighters were idiots, for lack of a better word, because they were constantly destroying evidence or overlooking a clear sign of arson and ruling it themselves as accidental. There was no short supply of ego on either side and it often led to conflicts and confrontations in the field and outside of it. I really hoped this wasn't going to blow up in my face, but I was keeping myself realistic at this point.

I knocked on my Captain's closed door. I waited until he granted me permission to enter. I sucked in a deep breath, bracing myself for the war that I was about to walk into. I opened the door and immediately closed it behind me.

I could see a quick flash of annoyance flicker through his eyes, not that I could blame him. We had gone a few rounds recently over these cases and I knew he already assumed that was why I was here. He was right, but that didn't make this any easier.

I didn't sit. I wanted to be standing and have some form of authority and power to my stance. He wasn't going to make me feel like I was wrong. He wasn't going to make me feel like I was crazy or out of line. Not this time. I had the evidence and this was going to happen, with or without his support.

"Investigator Cole, what do you want?"

He seemed stressed. The mountain of paperwork on his desk told me that he would be working all night to try and get it done. I knew he had been taking on more work because there were fewer Captains currently in the investigation unit. It happened, people moved, people get promoted, people left. The Upper Brass also didn't have the time to promote someone or knew who they might want to promote. The result was the rest of the Captains or Chiefs got the extra work to try and cover the person who had gone. They had no choice but to fill the gap and unfortunately, it resulted in a lot of work that the remaining people had to take on. I knew he was overworked, so I didn't take offense to his dismissive tone or that he seemed annoyed that I was there.

"I need to tell you something and I need you to be open-minded, Sir. I need you to understand that I wouldn't be coming to you with this if I didn't have solid evidence to back up what I'm claiming," I started, but before I could get much further he cut me off.

"If this is about those ghost cases you have been working on, the same cases I told you to shut down, you can walk out that door right now. I'm done with this, Cole, and I will not tell you again. We have enough cases in our backlog, I don't need you chasing down ones that are already closed."

We did have a large backlog, also a result of not having enough investigators, but the city wasn't looking to hire anymore. I knew this was going to be an uphill battle with him. I had mentioned these cases too many times to him and he was finally reaching his breaking point. But I couldn't walk away. I was way past that point and he needed to hear what I had to say, whether he liked it or not.

"Shelby Lewis, the fire at 467 Wilton Street yesterday. Her and her two young children were killed in a fire that was started by a device placed in the electrical panel. The same device that was responsible for starting the fire at Ms. Rollin's home two days ago. The same device that has been connected to thirty-five other cases. All thirty-five cases plus the most recent two cases, had cameras installed in the homes. All of them without those cameras being installed by the homeowners. The fire at Wilton Street, every battery was pulled from all of their smoke detectors," I continued, but once again he cut me off.

"I don't want to hear about any of these past cases. I'm sick to death of having to tell you the same thing. Having cameras in their home doesn't mean they are connected. They were investigated and solved."

I didn't let him finish. I continued on as if he didn't even interrupt me. I had to get this out before he kicked me out of there. The last thing I wanted to do was get into a shoving match with my Captain.

"The fire on Wilton Street had cameras, but they were newer. I took one of the cameras to Hank and he was able to get a serial number off of it. It traced back to the inventory at Spy Guy. Barba was able to get a warrant for the security footage and customer transaction list. Detective West served the warrant and I have spent the night going through security footage. Only one person used cash to purchase the cameras that were placed in the home." I pulled out the photo and placed it on his desk as I delivered the deadly blow. "Your brother. Taye. He purchased roughly a hundred of the small spy cameras."

He stared at me, now giving me his full attention. Gone was the anger from his eyes as he took the photo and looked at it. I knew what was coming and I had no way of giving him more proof than this. All I could do was hope I could get him to see the circumstantial evidence was too much to be a coincidence. I needed his help and I really hoped he would give it to me.

"He could have bought them for the firehouse. This doesn't prove anything," he rebutted as he tossed the photo back down onto his desk.

"He could, but that doesn't explain how one of the cameras he purchased ended up in a house that killed a widower and her two young children," I countered.

"They could have been stolen. You have no proof that he was there."

"With all due respect, Sir, you are not that stupid." I knew that was going to piss him off, but I didn't have time to tiptoe around the chain of command.

"Excuse me?" he snapped.

"Stop thinking like a Captain and start thinking like an investigator again. You used to be one of the best investigators in the fire department. There are multiple fires all with the same MO, all with the same cameras put up. One or two, maybe a coincidence, but thirty-seven, that we know of, that's a pattern, a signature and you know it. I found an old apartment building fire from twenty-five years ago with the same device and cameras found. I think it was the first fire to this arsonist. No one died, but he most likely lived there or knew someone who did. I know it wasn't Taye, he was too young, but I think whoever started the older fires mentored Taye and Taye set the last two fires at least.

He switched the cameras, most likely because he ran out of the other ones. They were discontinued fifteen years ago. These new cameras came with a server that isn't connected to the Internet. He would have that server somewhere with him. He has footage of the fire as he watched it."

"You don't know it's him. You only have him on camera purchasing small cameras. He could have used them at the firehouse. And I'm not saying these older fires aren't connected to each other, but we have no way to prove that. I understand it's personal to you with your parents' case, but we have no way to get evidence to reopen closed cases and investigate them for arson."

"Which is why I am pursuing the most recent cases that we have. It's a mentor and an apprentice. Taye is that apprentice and he could give us his mentor who we can speak with. You know arsonists like to lay claim to their work, they brag, we could get the cases closed if we get a confession. I know this is your brother, Cap. I don't like this anymore than you do. I don't want to stand here and tell you that your older brother is an arsonist. That your family's legacy is going to be destroyed by this. I don't want it to be a firefighter who does this, but the evidence is too hard to look away. You know he wouldn't need to purchase that many cameras for the firehouse. You know that no one would steal the cameras and use them to start a fire. And you know your brother, better than anyone. Are you really going to tell me, tell yourself, that there were no signs growing up? You know the signs of an arsonist; you know his behavior. You need to be honest with yourself so we can stop him before anyone else gets killed. He's already got at least four people that he's killed, including two children. I can stop him, but I can't without your help, Cap."

I really didn't know if he would. I prayed that he would, because I needed his help, I needed his support. He might be the only one who would be able to lead me to someone who could be the mentor in the relationship.

I could see the pain behind his eyes, the torment and conflict. He knew something, but he didn't know if he could admit to himself or to me. What I was asking him to do wasn't easy. I was asking him to betray not only his older brother, but his family's name. When this came out, it was going to be huge news and it wouldn't be long before every firehouse knew about it.

Before the Upper Brass knew about it.

This was going to cause him problems. He could very well be under investigation for it, too. It would be hard for people to believe that he knew nothing about what was going on. This was his only chance though, to prove that he was serious about his job, even if that meant that he had to help get his own brother arrested on arson charges.

He let out a deep sigh before he sat back in his chair and looked at me, meeting my eyes.

"Taye had always been odd growing up. He was six when he set fire to the carpet in the basement. It was small and our father was home and easily put it out. My mother was worried. He didn't really have friends and he wasn't social. She was worried that Taye's interest in fire was more than just a boy being a boy. My father thought that it was a good sign. He thought he was born to be a firefighter and he would make small controlled fires in the backyard with Taye. As he got older, Taye started to become disturbing. Around other people he was normal, but when he was home it was as if a switch had been flipped. I was terrified of him. We shared a room and I would spend all of my time out of it, even sleeping on the couch in the living room just so I didn't have to sleep around him. He got good at faking it around people."

"I've heard he has an issue with authority," I said as I absorbed everything that he had told me. It was all fitting with what an arsonist's profile was.

"Started with our father. The older he got, the more he wanted to do larger fires. He didn't want to have to wait for when my father was around for it. They often fought, sometimes physically. Taye barely made it through the fire academy, and the only reason he did was because my father and grandfather pulled some strings. He's never had respect for authority figures. He has always been very good at putting out fires. He's never held any fear of them. He's even done reckless things to help save someone."

"I know your father died in a fire roughly ten years ago at a storage facility. How has Taye been since then?" I suspected that was the stressor and Taye caused all the fires in the past ten years. I had no solid proof though, so I didn't want to bring that up just now.

"I saw him at our father's funeral. He seemed to be struggling and he was unstable. I justified it as him being upset over our father's death. Our mother had passed two years previously from cancer. I've barely seen him in the past decade. It's normally when we are going to the same conference or we happen to be at the same bar, and even then we only talk a small amount of time. I don't like being around him. He was close with our father. Our Dad seemed to be able to keep Taye in check, at least to a point. I think he always knew, though. He used to bring Taye in when he wasn't on shift to help run drills at different firehouses. He would have him set up the fire. I know our parents fought about it often. My mother didn't like that he was around fire so much and that our father was encouraging it. I think she always knew that he was born broken. My father only cared about fulfilling the legacy. It made it easier for him to ignore the signs or explain them away."

He ran a hand over his face and I could see that he was growing more tired as this conversation went on. I hated that I was adding to his stress, but there truly was nothing I could do about it. I needed some insight and answers and he was the only one who could give them to me.

"I'm sorry, Cap. This isn't how I wanted this case to go."

"It's not your fault. I should be the one apologizing. I shouldn't have dismissed your instinct with these cases. I should have taken the time to listen to you. Maybe if I had those people would still be alive, those kids would still be alive. We could have ended this years ago and maybe stopped Taye before he started his first fire. What do you need from me?"

I was relieved that he was willing to help me. That we had gotten over the initial shock and denial. Still though, that didn't ease my concerns that he would reach out to Taye and give him a head's up. They didn't appear to have much of a connection, and he seemed to understand how dangerous and sick his brother was, but that didn't change that sometimes blood was stronger than anything else in this world. All I could do was hope that he wouldn't reach out to Taye and tip him off.

"Was there anyone in his life that could have taken him on? Someone taught him about the cameras and the device. He would have been older, maybe had been burned himself."

"No, no one comes to mind, but like I said, we weren't that close. Captain William Clarke, he works out of the Twenty-First, they worked at the same firehouse ten years ago. He might have a better idea for you. You're going to speak with Taye?"

"I will be. For obvious reasons, you can't be involved in this, Cap. We need it clean for court."

"No, I understand. I'm not looking to put my hand in the cookie jar. He used to hide things in our bedroom in the closet under a floorboard. Old habits are hard to break, you might find the server there. Be careful though, he's not one to shy away from a fight and I don't need to tell you how dangerous arsonists are when they get backed into a corner," he warned.

"I know. I'll be careful, Sir. I'll make sure to go with a detective when I go and speak with him."

I wasn't about to put myself in a dangerous position. Besides, I had to have a detective there when he was being questioned to make it official. I also wasn't stupid. I was not about to walk into a dangerous situation with an unstable arsonist. Most tended to set themselves on fire to avoid going to jail. I wasn't about to put my life at risk like that.

"I need a favor from you."

"Of course." I assumed this was the part where he asked me to do this as quietly as possible.

"Pull the case file 45721, it's the fire from the storage facility that killed my father and two others. Taye, he was acting very differently at his funeral. Emotional like I had never seen him before. I could smell booze on his breath so I dismissed it, then. But looking back, he seemed guilty. This mentor, you suspect his first fire was an apartment building. It's possible that Taye's first fire was the storage facility. It was closed and marked accidental due to a short in the HVAC system. I've never had a reason to believe otherwise, but..." He opened his arms slightly toward his desk, his features twisting in resignation.

"I'll pull the file and look into it. The only way to get a solid answer might be through Taye, though."

"I know. Be careful."

"Always," I said, giving him a small nod before I turned on my heel and strode out of his office.

I now had someone else to speak to and hopefully, Captain Clarke would be able to give me more intel on Taye and who was around him ten years ago. I needed to try and find this mentor. I didn't even know if he was still alive, but if he was I had to find him. Getting to speak to him might be the only way I would be able to get justice for all of the people who lost their lives to him.

The only way I would be able to get

justice for my parents and myself.

I made my way out of the building and toward my car. I pulled out my phone and dialed Detective West. He wasn't going to be happy about this, but I knew he would have my back on it.

"Detective West."

"Hey, it's me, Tristan. I have a suspect on those arson cases for you. Lieutenant Taye Amaro. He works out of Station House Seventeen."

"A firefighter? You think he's behind all of these fires?" Detective West asked, obviously shocked, and I could hear the worry in his voice.

You didn't go against the blue line for the police, and you didn't go against the red line for the firefighters. They were brothers and they had no problem closing ranks to protect one of their own.

I knew I was potentially starting a war between not only the firefighters and the investigation division, but by asking Detective West to investigate him, it could be pitting cop against firefighter. It was a dangerous situation and it had to be handled very carefully.

"For the past ten years, including the two most recent fires. I believe he has a mentor who is responsible for the earlier fires. We have Taye on security footage purchasing, with cash, over a hundred of those cameras. I just spoke to his brother, my Captain, and he said that Taye has always had issues. That he started fires when he was six and has been unstable his whole life. Their father had been killed in a storage fire ten years ago. My Captain believes it's possible that could have been the first fire that Taye started. I'm going to pull the case file and review it. He didn't know of anyone who could have been a mentor, but he recommended that I speak with Captain Clarke, they were in the same firehouse at the time," I said as I climbed into my car.

"All right, I will start looking into Taye, quietly. You speak with Captain Clarke and let me know if he has someone in mind. I'll see if I can find someone on my end. I'll speak with ADA Barba about a search warrant for Taye's home."

That's what I loved about the detective. He didn't care if he was stepping foot into a war, he would do it in a heartbeat because it was the right thing to do. He never shied away from a tough case, even when it would have been in his best interest to. He was a good man and the reason why I always relied on him.

"Thanks, West. I know this puts you in a hard position."

"People are dead, kids are dead. That's the only thing that matters. Keep me posted."

"Will do," I said, before I ended the call.

Letting out a sigh, I cranked the ignition, shifted the car into gear and started to head toward firehouse Twenty-One. The only good thing about the impromptu visit was that I would get to see Hawke. That thought instantly warmed my heart and turned up the corners of my mouth, putting a smile on my face.

CHAPTER FOURTEEN

Hawke

I STROLLED INTO the Station House and immediately started toward where the bathroom was. I had been working on a rundown fire truck that Cap was hoping we could get started again. I wasn't the one who had experience with engines but I told him I would give it my best shot. I wasn't confident I could get it working again, but I was hopeful.

It had been a pretty slow day today, so far, thank fuck, but I also knew how quickly that could change. I had been hoping for a lighter day. I was feeling the fatigue of the past few days with pulling a lot of late nights working on the case with Tristan. I didn't regret it for a single second, but getting to sit for a little bit today would be nice. Hell, I was hoping to sneak a nap in later.

I couldn't stop the huge smile that spread over my face as I made my way into the main area and saw Tristan standing there. He looked very sexy wearing his suit, and what made it even better was knowing exactly how sexy he looked underneath it.

"Well, this is a nice surprise. What brings you by, Darlin'?"

"I spoke with my Captain and he recommended that I speak to your Captain. Apparently Captain Clarke and Taye worked in the same firehouse at the time of Taye's father's death."

"How did it go?" I asked, with a nod toward the hallway as I started to walk toward the bathroom.

"As well as could be expected. He was angry at first, but he came around. According to him, Taye started making fires at six and he's always been disturbing. Their father didn't want to see it, but apparently his mother did. I truly don't believe he knew what Taye was doing. He has barely seen him in ten years, since their father's funeral. I called Detective West and he's going to look into Taye. My Captain also wants me to look into the storage facility fire that killed their father. He is now wondering if Taye started the fire. I'll look into it, but I might not be able to find anything to pinpoint it to Taye."

"That might be impossible, unless he wants to admit to it, but even if he does there's no way to know if he's being honest. That might be something your Captain has to live without knowing for certain. Hopefully, Cap might know someone you can speak to."

"Where is everyone? It's pretty quiet in here."

"Cap is actually out meeting with someone and he won't be back for about forty minutes or so. The rest of the guys are outside running drills. I was working on an old engine that Cap is hoping I can get started," I said as I walked into the bathroom. "Care to shower with me?"

I asked over my shoulder, flashing him a sexy smirk.

I really hoped he would say yes. I would have loved to be able to get my hands on him again, but there was no pressure. It was completely his call to make.

"What if someone walks in?"

"No one will. They just started a drill, so they'll be busy for an hour, easily. It's completely up to you," I said as I reached to pull my t-shirt over my head.

"He says, as he gets naked," he teased with a grin plastered on his face.

"What? I need a shower," I said with a wink and a playful smile.

"We're gonna get in trouble."

"That's part of the fun," I said, with a chuckle before I stepped into the shower, turning the water on so it was nice and hot.

It was only a minute later when the door opened and a very naked Tristan stepped in. The second he was inside with me, I pulled him in for a kiss. He effortlessly pressed his lips right back on mine and I deepened the kiss. He moaned and ran his calloused hands over my chest as he felt my tongue tangle with his.

I moved my hands down the curves of his back and over his ass. He had a great ass. I pulled him closer to me until both of our hard dicks rubbed against each other, causing us both to moan into the kiss. We started to grind against each other as the pleasure overtook our bodies.

He was like gasoline to the fire that was spreading through my body and it was one fire I never wanted to put out.

Tristan was the first one to break away from the kiss. He pressed open-mouthed kisses over my skin, making his way down my chest and over my stomach as he got down onto his knees. I watched, my breath hitching in my chest as he ran his tongue along my hard shaft from my balls to the slit. I couldn't contain the rush of air that left my lips as I watched him open his luscious lips and suck my tip into his hot mouth.

We didn't get to do this last time. Last time, I was much more interested in exploring his body. This time, it seemed like he wanted to discover more of mine and I was more than happy to let him explore away.

Tristan hummed his appreciation as

he sucked on the head of my cock and I throbbed in his mouth. I couldn't help but thread my fingers through his hair, gripping it tight as electricity and heat washed trough me when he tongued my slit. I placed my hand on the back of his head, holding him in place as he wrapped his fist around the base of my dick and moved his mouth down to take in more of my hardness.

I knew that I was a very good size and it wasn't simple for someone to take all of me in their mouth so I really didn't expect it from Tristan. I couldn't take my gaze off of him as he worked my dick in his mouth, taking more and more with each pass. As he opened his throat and sucked me down, I couldn't help but lightly thrust my hips toward his mouth. It was a knee jerk reaction to the pleasure that was creeping up my spine and the feel of his throat closing over my hard shaft. I was pleasantly rewarded with a deep, rumbling sound that came from Tristan's chest and sent all kinds of new feelings racing through me. I knew it was safe for me to do it again, that he would welcome my taking control.

I *needed* to hear that sound again.

I started to lightly thrust into Tristan's willing mouth and I moaned right along with him, the pleasure building in my stomach.

"Tris," I hissed out, as he again pulled up toward the tip and then hollowed his cheeks as he sucked me all the way down to my base, his other hand fingering my balls as they pulled up tight.

The sounds of intense enjoyment kept

coming from Tristan, groans and growls, humming and whimpering, and they were driving me insane, ramping up the pleasure thrice fold. That he could appear to take such amazing pleasure in giving oral sex as much as I was enjoying receiving it blew my mind.

I felt his hands moving around to cup my ass and he pulled me closer, making sure that I stayed deep in his mouth as I continued to shuttle in and out of his throat even faster now. It didn't take long before I let loose a deep groan as I snapped my hips forward and buried myself completely in his mouth, coming down his throat.

Tristan moaned and greedily swallowed every last drop that I had for him, moving up to suck my sensitive tip clean.

I quickly pulled him off my cock and yanked him onto his feet, capturing his mouth with mine all over again. Instantly, his tongue was tangling with mine and I could taste myself as our tongues danced once again.

The contact was nowhere near enough for either one of us. I moved my hands to cup the bottom of his ass and picked him up. Tristan wrapped his legs around my hips as I moved us so his back was against the wall of the shower. I held him up as I reached for the shampoo and poured some on my already hard dick and three fingers before I slipped two fingers into Tristan's waiting hole. He let out a deep grunt into the kiss at the rapid invasion and started to rock his hips back and forth, fucking himself on my fingers as heady whimpers escaped his throat.

I could feel how urgent and needy he was so I worked my fingers in and out of him quickly as I focused on stretching him enough so we could have sex without causing him any pain. I quickly slipped in a third finger and searched out that bundle of nerves that would make Tristan scream. He broke from the kiss and let out a hoarse cry, arching his back from the pleasure as I swiped over his sweet spot.

I smirked as I pressed my mouth along his neck, licking the salty taste from his skin as I hit the same spot again.

Tristan wrapped his arms around my shoulders and rocked against my fingers inside of him.

"Oh god, Hawke. Make me yours.

Please." He whimpered, moving his hips back and forth rapidly, grinding his ass down on my digits.

"You want to be mine?" I lightly teased as I sucked gently on his neck, being careful to not leave a mark.

"Oh fuck yes, please, fill me now," he begged.

That was all I needed to hear. I removed my fingers from his hole and quickly notched the tip of my dick into place, hesitating only briefly. I knew that I should be wearing a condom, we both did, but right now that wasn't important. We both wanted this. I knew he wanted it when he asked me to make him mine. Firefighters had regular testing as part of the health and wellness program, so I knew I was clean and I had no doubt that he was as well.

I started to gently push myself into his sweet ass. Tristan let out a soft moan as I breached his tight ring of muscles. We had just had sex last night, but he felt just as amazing as he did the first time.

Maybe even more.

I pressed inside of him until I was balls deep in his tight, hot ass. His walls felt glorious around my dick and I never wanted to leave. I would have been happy to spend all day and night buried deep inside of him. Without the barrier of the condom, the sensation was even more intense.

"Oh, you feel so good," I said, my voice betraying me as I fought to control myself.

"Move, and don't hold back," Tristan begged.

I did not need to be told twice. I was happy to know that Tristan felt just as much in need as I was. I pulled back almost all the way before I slammed back in, causing Tristan to let out a whimper as he moved his hips to try and get the right angle.

I knew I hit his sweet spot on the next thrust when Tristan tossed his head back and let loose a small scream from the pleasure scorching through his body.

"Your delicious pleasure sounds are driving me crazy," I growled out, my voice breathy and gravelly as I rocketed my hips back and forth, pounding even harder into him. I moved my mouth over his skin, the salty taste of him flooding over my tongue and adding to the building euphoria.

I had never felt this good before. I

couldn't even describe how remarkable it felt with my bare cock buried deep inside him. There were no words. I knew sex felt great, but I had no idea it could ever feel like this.

Sex with Tristan was earth shattering and I never wanted it to end.

I knew we were only going to have time to do this once, but I would have loved to do this a hundred times. Hell, a thousand times.

We were going at his pace, but I knew I was never going to be satisfied with having just a casual fling with Tristan. My body would want more, just like my heart would.

I made sure that my dick hit Tristan's sweet spot dead on with each thrust. I could feel his legs trembling with need. I could feel his ass getting tighter, his walls squeezing my dick and ramping up my pleasure to a whole new level.

"Fuck, I'm close, don't stop," he begged, as he clenched his hands on my shoulders, his nails embedded in my skin. They were going to leave marks but I didn't care. In fact, the light pain as they broke the skin sent my mind soaring.

I picked up my pace even more, giving him everything that I had to offer. I was close as well and I wanted—no, I *needed* to feel him come. I needed to feel his walls tightening around my dick without a condom to dull the pleasure.

I moved my mouth along his neck, my tracing the shell of his ear with my tongue before I whispered. "Come for me, Darlin'."

Tristan whined, bucking back against

my thrusts as his orgasm inched closer. I could feel his ass tightening around my dick and after two more direct hits against his prostate, Tristan let out a loud moan as he started to come, his hot seed spreading between us, coating my belly and his.

I loved knowing that I could push him over the edge without even touching his dick. The knowledge sent a heady spike of pleasure through my brain and the tightening of his muscles around my dick only pushed me over the edge.

I slammed my hips forward and buried my cock inside of Tristan as I erupted with a long, throaty moan.

Tristan let out a soft moan as I continued to paint his walls with my heat. I had never come inside of someone before, never had sex without a condom, and I knew in that moment I was addicted to the sensation.

We were both breathing heavily as we continued to pulse. I lightly began to kiss Tristan as we both tried to catch our breath. We kissed for a few moments before I started to feel Tristan's lips not pressing as hard against my own. I could feel his body getting weaker and I knew we needed to get out of the shower. The water was hot and the heat was clearly getting to him.

I pulled back from the kiss and placed my hand on the side of his face as I spoke.

"You okay, Darlin'?"

"Ah... yeah. Just starting to get light headed. I think the heat and exertion is getting to me," he said with a warm goofy smile covering his features.

I let him gradually slide down my body until his feet touched the floor, but I kept my arm wrapped tightly around his waist as I reached over and turned the water off. I carefully helped him climb out of the shower stall and wrapped a towel around him before sitting him down on one of the benches.

"Thanks. I haven't eaten since breakfast and I didn't eat yesterday. My blood sugar level is likely quite mad at me."

"You do that often?" I asked, worried about his physical health. It wasn't safe to be skipping meals.

"Sometimes, more often than I should, if I'm being honest. I can get lost in the cases that I'm working on and next thing I know it's been sixteen hours and I haven't moved from my desk. I'm trying to get better with it. Sometimes I remember to set an alarm on my phone so I come up for air," he said with a small shrug and a light chuckle.

"You have to be careful. You need to eat more than once a day, Darlin'," I chastised as I tugged on my clothes.

"I know. It's a work in progress," he said, as he started rub the towel over his flushed skin.

I kept my gaze on him as he got dressed. I wanted to make sure he didn't fall over or get dizzy. I knew we should be talking about the fact that I didn't wear a condom, but I doubted here and now was the best place or time for it. Still, it was a conversation that we really should have.

"Real quick, I know I didn't wear a condom. I'm clean and I know I should have asked," I started, but Tristan cut me off.

"You didn't have to ask, I said it first. You knew what I meant and I'm clean, too. I might not know your favorite food or color, but I do know that you would never put me at risk like that if you weren't clean as well."

The fact that he could say that so confidently told me that he knew me better than most people. He knew that I would never put anyone in that kind of danger or position.

The way our bodies connected, the way it seemed like we knew one another so well, it was cosmic. We *had* to have known each other before this life. I was convinced of it.

With us both dressed, I went over to him and pulled him in for a quick kiss. I didn't get to kiss him anywhere near the length of time that I wanted to, but I knew we couldn't get caught in the bathroom together. It wasn't a big deal for us to be seen together or to be seen kissing. But I didn't want the guys to meet Tristan in the bathroom with me for the first time as the announcement of our relationship. I also didn't want to rush Tristan. He was out, but he wasn't screaming from a rooftop about it. I had to take things slow and wait until he was comfortable. Unlike the other guys that I'd dated who wanted to live in their carefully constructed closets, I knew that Tristan would be okay with going public one day.

I just knew it in my heart.

I pulled back after a moment and flashed him a warm smile.

"Come on, Cap might be back now."

I guided him out of the bathroom and I went and poked my head around the corner to see if Cap was back in. I wasn't sure he would be, but sure enough he was back in his office. A brief thought flickered through my mind that he might have heard us in the bathroom, but I dismissed it. If he had heard anyone having sex, he would have been standing outside the bathroom door waiting to see who walked out.

"He's back. And no, he wouldn't have heard us," I said with a smirk, already knowing what he was going to say.

"You sure?" he asked, his face slightly flushed.

"Yes, trust me. Come on, let's see if we can get you that mentor's name." The sooner we wrapped this case up, the sooner I could try and help Tristan move on from his childhood trauma.

We headed over to Captain Clarke's office. He had the door open and he looked up when he heard us approach.

"Hey Cap, do you have a minute?" I asked, but I knew he would say he did. He was always like that. Even if he was drowning in work, if one of his guys came up to him and asked to talk, he always said yes.

"Always. Close the door," he said as he went and sat down in his seat.

I closed the door as I spoke. "You remember Investigator Cole."

"Of course. How are you, Cole?"

"I'm doing well, Sir. I'm hoping you will be able to help with the investigation into the Rollins' fire as well as the Lewis' fire from yesterday."

"I'm always happy to help, though, I don't know how much help I'll be."

"One of the cameras from the Lewis' fire, we were able to get a serial number off of it. We traced it back to Spy Guy, a store that caters to private detectives and spy enthusiasts. We were able to get a warrant for the security footage and customer transaction lists. We were able to find the suspect that purchased a bulk order of the cameras, Lieutenant Taye Amaro."

I kept my eyes on Cap. I had to see what his reaction would be. I hadn't known he worked with Taye in the past until my Captain mentioned it and I had no idea what his stance on him was. Tristan had already had to argue with one Captain today; I was really hoping he wouldn't have to battle with another one.

"You think he's an arsonist. Have you spoken with his brother yet?" Captain Clarke said. I couldn't get a read on his emotions, though. His tone stayed the same, his facial features betraying nothing.

"I just came from there. He's my Captain and it was a shock, but at the same time it wasn't. He recommended that I speak with you. I think Taye is the apprentice. I believe his mentor is responsible for over two dozen fires over the past twenty-five years. Including the fire that killed my parents and almost killed me."

"I'm sorry to hear that. I had no idea," Cap piped up, sympathy lacing his voice.

"It's not something I broadcast. We think the death of his father ten years ago was the stressor that pushed his desire as a firebug into an active status. Captain Amaro is also having me look into the fire that killed his father, he is now wondering if it was Taye's first arson attempt. I was hoping though, that you might remember someone older that was around Taye. Someone who could have been a mentor to him."

"I never liked Taye. I always got a bad vibe off of him. He didn't have much in the way of friends. Some of the guys would hang around him because he was a legacy and they hoped to get some of that rubbed off on them. There was one guy though, Wilson Stan. He used to come around a couple times a week. It wasn't to just see Taye, though. He hung around all the time. He used to work at the firehouse, but about twenty-six, twenty-seven years ago he was injured really badly in a factory fire. Both of his legs sustained third degree burns and were broken from a steel shelving unit falling on him. He was medically released, placed on long-term disability. He was twenty-eight at that point, I believe. He's about fifty-five, now."

"He would have been thirty at the time of the apartment fire. More than old enough to start setting fires. It would have been a year, maybe two years, since the fire he was injured in. Plenty of time for his legs to heal. And they were around each other often?" I asked.

Wilson sounded like our guy. He would have the experience and knowledge of starting fires. He was around Taye and could have easily spoken to him after his father's death.

Not to mention these guys knew each other. Arsonists have a way of sniffing out other arsonists like their lives depended on it. Wilson could have easily discovered Taye's desires and started to groom him.

"A few times a week, and that is just what I know of. They could have easily met outside of the firehouse. Whenever people came around and saw Taye, he was stoic, as if being normal took every ounce of strength he had. But with Wilson, he came alive. They would go off and talk to each other for hours and Taye hung on Wilson's every word. Taye was practically obsessed with him."

"That sounds like our guy. I'll give Detective West a call and let him know. Thank you, Captain," Tristan said, flashing the other man a friendly smile.

"You're welcome. I hope you get the evidence that you need to put them both behind bars. If there is anything you need from me, please don't hesitate to ask," Captain Clarke said.

"I will, thank you," Tristan responded.

"I'll walk you out," I offered.

He gave me a nod and we both headed out of the Captain's office. I was starting to feel excited knowing that we now had both of our suspects figured out. However, I was also worried because now Tristan was going to have to hunt them down and that could be very dangerous.

I walked him outside before I decided to speak. I knew his mind would be going a mile a minute and he might appreciate the quiet couple of minutes.

"You won't be going after them alone,

right?" I inquired.

"No. I'll give Detective West a call and he'll look into Wilson. I'll be there when they go after them, but I won't be in any danger. We've done this before. I let the strong men with the guns handle things," he quipped with a teasing smirk.

"You joke, but I'm glad that there are strong men with guns when you are around arsonists. Please let me know when you go in and come out so I know you are safe."

I had no right to ask that of him, but I hoped he would give me a break for asking. We weren't official, we were friends and even that was new. Still, I was going to worry about him until I knew that he was safe.

"I will. I'll be fine, don't worry. Am I

going to see you after work tonight, or do you need to get some real sleep for a change?"

"Who says I can't get sleep with you?" I countered.

"The two hours of sleep we got last night would dictate otherwise."

"Well, I'm willing to try again if you are."

I knew he usually had a hard time sleeping anyway, but I hoped that with finding his suspects it might be a bit easier on him. And if not, I had no problem holding him all night long even if we didn't get much sleep.

"Okay, text me after your shift."

"I will. Be safe."

"You, too," he said, before he turned and strolled off to his car.

I had no choice but to watch as he

walked away. I had no choice but to hope and pray that when I saw him tonight that he would be okay. One thing I did know, if Taye or Wilson tried to hurt him, it would be them getting burned up in a fire next.

CHAPTER FIFTEEN

Tristan

I PULLED UP to Taye's house and parked across from it. I had called Detective West before I left the firehouse and he was able to easily find Taye's address. He was registered with the Fire Department and Human Resources needed updated addresses and contact information for everyone who was being paid by the city, so finding that information was a breeze.

I had hoped he would be able to locate Wilson as well, but with the older man no longer being with the department, it was going to be harder to track him down. He was getting disability, but he could have it set up as an automatic deposit and email updates so he didn't have to have mail going to a physical address. Any address on file with the disability office could be a decade old.

I knew we would find him eventually, it was only a matter of time, but that didn't change the fact that I didn't want him to go out and find someone new to mentor and we'd then have this whole process to start all over again.

I climbed out of my car and made my

way over to Detective West. He had arrived not too long before me and he was waiting for me so we could question Taye together. This was going to be a touchy conversation. We had enough to arrest Taye on. We might not be able to charge him, yet, but we could hold him for forty-eight hours while we cleared the warrants and grabbed solid evidence. It would also give us the chance to interrogate him, and if he was like other arsonists, he'd talk.

"Any luck finding Wilson Stan?" I asked, once I was close enough.

"Not yet. No address on file and his cell phone isn't in service any longer. It's going to take some work to track him down, but we might be able to get something from Taye."

"Assuming he is feeling chatty."

"Let's hope. I don't want to kick the door down, so it would be better if he felt like we were going to him for help on a case. It should get us in the door without any confrontation. I got the arrest warrant, but it would be easier if he played ball, though. The last thing I want to do is start a war between the PD and FD."

That I could understand fully. We were walking a very dangerous fine line right now and the last thing we needed was a war between our two departments. We had to tread carefully and the best way to prevent World War Three would be to get Taye to come in on his own accord.

I gave him a nod and we made our way over to the front door. Detective West knocked and we waited a moment before it finally opened. Taye stood on the other side of the door and I could tell he wasn't surprised to see us, but he faked it. He had to have known it was coming at some point. Somewhere along the way, he had to have known that he would get caught, either him or Wilson. It was hard enough to stay going for long periods of time as an arsonist; it was even harder to keep two arsonists working together under wraps.

"Lieutenant Amaro, my name is Detective West and this is Investigator Cole. We would like to come in and speak with you for a moment about a case we are currently investigating."

"Of course, I am always happy to help," Taye said with a forced smile.

I knew he was trying to play a game. It was the only thing he could do. He couldn't turn us away. It would look suspicious. He would also want to know what we knew. We weren't the only ones walking a fine line. All I could do was hope that we knew how to walk it better than he did.

He stepped back and allowed us to enter. I didn't see anything that stood out as dangerous. One could never tell when they went to a suspect's home what they would find. I had walked into places that were filled with explosives and bomb making materials completely left out in the open. It was like people believed that we wouldn't arrest them for things in plain sight.

We made our way into the living room, but before I could even sit down on the couch, Detective West let out a grunt before he collapsed to the floor. I snapped my eyes up to see Wilson standing behind where Detective West was with a gun in his hand.

I held my hands up slightly as I risked a quick glance down at Detective West. He was out cold. There was some blood on the back of his head and given that I hadn't heard a gunshot, I assumed that Wilson had pistol-whipped him. I hoped he would be okay. I knew head injuries were hard to gauge and something as simple as getting hit on the back of the head could cause swelling and bleeding, both of which could kill him if I didn't get us out of this soon.

"Tie him up," Wilson snapped to Taye, and it was clear he was furious that we were here.

I couldn't blame him, he had gone for

twenty-five years, a quarter of a century undetected, and now he was going to be arrested along with Taye, because Taye had screwed up with the new cameras.

Wilson kept the gun pointed at me as Taye approached me. I could fight, sort of, but there was no way I would be able to take on Taye and Wilson together, especially when Wilson had a gun. I didn't doubt for a single second that the man wouldn't be afraid to fire it.

Taye grabbed my right arm and pulled me over to the kitchen that was in plain view of the front door. He grabbed one of the wooden chairs from under the dining room table and forced me down into it.

I watched helplessly as Wilson grabbed Detective West by the back of his shirt and dragged him over so he was closer to me, but not close enough so I could reach out with my foot and touch him. I knew he had done it so it was easier to keep an eye on both of us.

Taye quickly zip-tied my wrists to the arms of the chair before he stepped back, appearing to be satisfied with himself.

This was not how I had imagined my day going. I didn't know what I had expected, but it wasn't this when we came here to speak and arrest Taye. With Detective West now out of commission, it was on me to try and get Taye and Wilson to come in peacefully.

I knew they wouldn't, though.

Trying to talk them down would be like trying to walk an unstable homemade bomb across a rickety bridge with missing planks.

One wrong step and everything went boom.

"How the hell did you let this happen?" Wilson snapped at Taye.

He wasn't happy about the situation and it made sense. He had gone for so long not being caught and now his carefully constructed world was falling down around him and there was nothing he could do about it. The situation was out of his control and for an arsonist that was a major issue. They hated not having control.

"I didn't do anything wrong," Taye instantly denied.

"If you didn't do anything wrong, then they wouldn't be here. They clearly have figured this out. You screwed up somewhere. Over twenty years I have never been suspected by a single cop,"

Wilson seethed.

"It was the cameras," I stated. I didn't really want to listen to them arguing back and forth about whose fault it was. It was one thing to try and buy time, but no one was going to come for us. It wasn't like someone would be checking up on Detective West if he didn't check in within the hour.

"What about the cameras?" Wilson asked, looking right at Taye.

"Nothing. They were perfect."

"They were new. The switch between the old cameras that were untraceable to the new ones led me right to you. They didn't burn up in the fire, leaving a serial number behind that I traced back to the store where they were purchased. I got the security footage and found Taye. Then it was just a matter of talking to people who knew Taye to find you," I explained.

I wasn't sure how this was going to end, but all I could hope for was that I could make them turn against each other and then somehow figure out how to get out of there. The chair I was restrained in was wood, so I could break it if I got the chance to. The trick was getting the chance. They were both unstable, no matter how well they had been able to fake it; they were unstable and unpredictable. The new intel only pissed Wilson off. He pistol whipped Taye across the face as he spoke.

"You stupid son of a bitch. I told you to never use new cameras. You were supposed to only use the one brand. They were untraceable."

"They were garbage cameras. They

didn't last long enough from the heat. The new cameras stay intact longer, letting me watch them die longer."

"And I told you new cameras last longer in the heat making them easier to trace. How could you be this stupid? Now we have no way of knowing how many people know about us. I taught you better than this. I taught you to be smarter than this. I thought you had what it took to be one of the best, but I was clearly wrong. You're a disgrace and disappointment."

"I'm a disappointment? You're the old man who couldn't start a fire anymore. You have to rely on me to give you the footage just so you can jerk off to it. You're the disgrace," Taye seethed.

I knew what was going to happen before it even did. Wilson was the first to make a move. He went to raise his gun, but Taye punched him and pushed the gun out of his hands. It didn't take long at all before Wilson recovered and charged toward Taye, wrapping his arms around his waist and pushing him down to the ground.

While they were busy fighting each other, I turned my attention to trying to get out of this chair. I pulled against the zip ties to try and break them. They were tight and they were already cutting into my skin. The chair was stronger than I had expected. I thought it would be easy to break, but with the zip ties being so tight, I wasn't able to get enough slack to pull my wrists back far enough to hit the chair with any real force.

The echo of a gunshot pulled my attention back over to Wilson and Taye.

Wilson was on top of Taye and they were both on the floor. I couldn't see the gun, so I had no idea who had been shot or where they were shot. I kept my eyes locked on them, waiting to see which one of them would move.

After a second, Wilson's body moved, but he wasn't the one controlling it.

Taye pushed Wilson's body off of him and I was able to see the large blood stain growing on Wilson's chest. He wasn't moving and his eyes were open, but they were blank. He was dead and I couldn't feel upset about it. I was upset that I wouldn't be able to question him, but I knew in my gut that he was responsible for my parents' death.

Taye stood and he didn't even appear shaken by the fact that he'd just killed a man. His mentor. He had the man's blood all down the front of him and yet, he looked at Wilson as if he was just some bug he had stepped on.

I knew there was only one way this was going to go.

Taye was going to do what every arsonist did.

He was going to start a fire.

I could see the gears turning in his mind, deciding on how he wanted to do it. He was angry at the situation that he was in. I knew he wasn't able to feel emotions, so losing his mentor wouldn't affect him the same way it would for a normal person.

For Taye, it was just another body.

He had outgrown his mentor, surpassed him, and improved on the techniques that he had been taught. It had only been a matter of time before they'd butted heads and one of them died anyway. This was why arsonists don't work in pairs. They didn't like to compromise on their processes and they didn't like sharing the pleasure that they got from the fires they started. It was honestly a miracle that Willson and Taye had managed to get along for the ten years they had.

"Taye, listen to me," I started. I had to try and get him to see reason, or at least some self-preservation.

"Shut up. You have nothing that I want to hear," Taye snapped before he turned on his heel and strode quickly out of the room.

The second I was alone, I resumed my struggles against the zip ties. I had to get us out of here. Detective West hadn't even so much as twitched since he went down. The only reason I knew he was still alive was the subtle movement of his chest. I took comfort in seeing his chest rising and falling, but it would have been more comforting if he was awake and talking. At least then he would be able to help me get out of here. Instead, it was up to me and so far, I couldn't even get out of the damn chair.

Taye came back into the room far sooner than I would have liked. He clearly knew what he wanted to do, so it hadn't taken him long to grab the gas can from his garage.

I continued my struggles against the zip ties. No amount of talking was going to change what he was about to do. Taye was ready to die there today and he was going to take us all with him.

When I heard the liquid splashing the

floor, I snuck a quick glance his way. He was pouring the gas all over Wilson's body and around the kitchen. He was going to make sure that Wilson burned up first, but it wasn't out of respect for the man. This was his way of giving his dead mentor one last *fuck you* by killing him a second time.

My gaze went to Taye as he pulled out a zippo lighter. With a flick of his thumb the flame came to life.

CHAPTER SIXTEEN

Hawke

WE HAD MANAGED to make it through most of the day before we got a call. It was better than getting calls back to back and if it was a slow day, at least that meant less people were being hurt. This was another residential fire and I couldn't help but wonder if the fire would be connected to Taye and Wilson, or if this one was a true accident.

Before this case, I'd never wondered how the fire got started. I was always focused on making sure anyone who was trapped inside got out and that we got the fire out before there was nothing left of the house. Now, my thoughts immediately went to arson and I knew it was going to take some time before my mind went back to normal.

"Here we go, boys!" Gage called out from the front seat as we pulled up to the fire.

I put my gloves on and got ready to climb out of the truck. The second we stopped, we all tumbled out of the truck and took in the scene. The flames were starting to come out of the windows on both floors and I knew right away by the smoke color that an accelerant had been used. I scanned the area to make sure everyone who was outside was far enough away to remain safe. A couple of cop cars were already there and they had started to evacuate the homes that were around the fire. My heart dropped to the pit of my stomach as my gaze landed on a car that I knew.

Tristan was here.

If Tristan was here, that meant that this house had to belong to either Taye or Wilson, and that meant he was in the house.

"Hey, we got a detective's squad car over here!" Zander called out.

"It's gotta be Detective West's car. He was working with Investigator Cole in an arson case. Cole's car is here, too. They have to be in the house," I informed them as I ran over to join the rest of them.

Everything in me was screaming for me to run into the house and save him. I didn't care if I had a hose or not, I needed to get to him. I had to make sure he was safe. He was trapped in another fire and he had to be scared.

I couldn't believe this was happening. I didn't even think it would happen when he went to speak with Taye or Wilson. I'd foolishly believed that he would be safe, because Detective West would be with him.

I should have known better.

I should have told him to wait and go with a fire engine on standby just in case either one of them started a fire to get out of being arrested. I should have done more and now Tristan might be paying for my mistakes.

Before anymore could be said, we saw a man running out of the house and I instantly knew it was Taye. I was not about to let him get away with this.

"Grab him!" I yelled.

I didn't know who would listen to me, but with enough firefighters and cops there, I figured someone would. Two local patrol officers that I didn't know grabbed him and tackled him to the ground, and all that mattered to me at that moment was that he had been caught.

"He's a firefighter," Gabe instantly said, shock filling his voice. But he had no idea what type of firefighter Taye really was. Thankfully, before I had to be the one to say it, Cap did.

"Arrest him. He's suspected in multiple arson investigations, including this house."

I could see the shock on all of the guys' faces, minus Zander's. I knew it was going to be shocking and I knew most wouldn't want to believe it, but it was the reality that we faced. Taye was an arsonist who was responsible for multiple deaths and he was not about to get away with it.

"Get the hose lines going, we've got two men in there!" Cap yelled and got everyone to snap back into focus.

I watched as the cops took Taye, struggling and running his mouth about it being a lie, over to their patrol car. They would have to take him to the hospital to get checked out, but right now he was being handled. With Taye under control for the time being, I didn't even waste a second before I threw on my oxygen mask and ran toward the house.

Zander came right behind me.

I ignored the shout from Captain Clarke demanding I had to go in with a hose. I was not about to let Tristan stay in the house a moment longer. He was already in danger and any delay, even just a second, could be fatal and that was not something I was willing to accept.

The moment we were in the house I was scanning every room. I had to find him. Tristan was here and he had to be terrified. It was bad enough he had already been trapped in a fire as a child, but to have to experience it again. He wasn't mentally recovered from the first fire and now he would have more trauma to pile on top of the already existing trauma.

The fire was burning hot and flames licked at my suit, the heat almost overwhelming as thick black smoke billowed throughout the room. Taye had obviously used some type of accelerant.

That was the problem when you confronted an arsonist, they always prefered to go down in their own fire. They didn't like being kept in a cell or locked up unable to indulge in their compulsion. We had Taye, but I had no idea if Wilson would be there as well. We also had to try and find Detective West.

I was trying to ignore the likelihood that Detective West and Tristan were already dead, either from the heat or the smoke. With Tristan already having been in a fire where there was smoke inhalation, I was worried about what it could do to his lungs a second time around. I knew from other firefighters who'd had to go in without a mask, breathing in the toxic fumes, it had a way of eating at your lungs. The more often it happened, the longer the recovery time took.

Keeping low, I walked into the kitchen area and instantly my heart went up to my throat. I vaguely picked up Detective West's body where it lay unmoving on the floor. All I could see in that moment was Tristan tied to a chair, unconscious. There were flames all around him and quickly approaching his chair. If we had been another minute longer and he would have been on fire.

I hastily crossed the distance between us and though it violated protocol, I pulled off my mask and placed it over his face. I grabbed my clippers and cut the zip ties that kept him bound to the chair. I briefly caught sight of Zander grabbing Detective West and carrying him out. I hoped the man would be okay.

I knew Tristan would blame himself if the detective didn't make it. It wouldn't be his fault, but that wouldn't matter to Tristan. It was his case and that would be enough for him to place all the blame on his own shoulders. I couldn't think about that right now. All that mattered was getting Tristan out of there safe.

I picked him up in my arms and ran as quickly as I could out of the house. The smoke was already burning my lungs and I had only been without my mask for less than two minutes.

The second I was out of the house

and able to take a breath of fresh air, I couldn't help but cough. The smoke had been so thick in the house it didn't take long before it restricted my breathing. I carried Tristan over to the first stretcher and Newt instantly removed my mask from Tristan's face and replaced it with an oxygen mask. I faintly registered that the paramedic was speaking to me.

"You need to get checked out. That smoke is thick."

"I'm fine. He was in a fire twenty-one years ago. His lungs might be weakened from it."

"I got him," Newt promised.

Newt was one of our more recent paramedics, he had been with us for two weeks now and he seemed like a good guy. He was a bit different, nerdy and not what one would expect for a paramedic. He was thin, but he ate all the time. He was never far from a package of M&Ms. I didn't know much about him, none of us really did. He liked comic books, he was always reading one. Outside of that, I knew nothing about him. That wasn't unusual with paramedics. They came and went so many times it was hard to keep track. According to Zander, we used to have the same paramedics for years, but the city wanted them to float so they could constantly have enough in each firehouse. Most were also female and the city was constantly worried about relationships occurring between the paramedics and the firefighters and sexual harassment suits becoming a problem. Apparently, the city felt it was easier to make them rotate than to expect for the men who worked around them to behave themselves.

I had no choice but to watch as Newt had to intubate Tristan. I had no alternative but to stand by and do nothing as Newt, a man I hardly knew, worked to help the man that I was falling in love with. I had to trust that Tristan would be okay.

I had never felt so helpless before in my entire life and there had been plenty of times in my life where I couldn't help someone. I'd never expected to be put in the position to feel powerless when it came to someone that I cared about. I'd foolishly believed that nothing bad would ever happen to someone I cared for. It was childish and naive, but it helped me to feel better to believe that I would never have to be the one sitting next to a hospital bed. I would never have to be the one in the waiting room pacing around and hoping someone in a set of scrubs told me something good.

I saw horrible things every day. I saw people on the worst day of their lives frequently. Sometimes it was from a fire and sometimes from a horrible accident. And yet, I'd never expected for any of that to happen to me, to someone I knew. I had managed to convince myself that it couldn't possibly to happen to me or someone I loved.

I had just gotten one hell of a dose of reality and I didn't like it.

"Is he going to be okay?" I tried to make sure my voice didn't shake as I spoke, but I could tell by the flash of concern that moved across Newt's eyes that I hadn't succeeded.

HAWKE

"It's hard to say with smoke inhalation. Doctors at Mercy will have a better guess for you. We gotta move," Newt answered as he pushed the stretcher into the back of the ambulance.

I looked back over at the house, at the guys as they were still fighting to put the fire out. I should be back over there helping them, but my whole body was screaming for me to get into the back of that ambulance and never leave Tristan's side. I was on duty and it wouldn't be appropriate for me to just up and leave in the middle of a call, in the middle of my shift. The guys all knew that I was gay, but they didn't know about Tristan. He wasn't hiding, but he didn't broadcast it and right now was not the ideal time to do so.

At the same time though, how could I leave him alone?

What if he didn't make it?

I couldn't leave him to take his last breaths around a bunch of strangers that barely knew his name. He deserved better than that.

"Hawke!"

I looked over at Captain Clarke. I knew what he was going to say, that I needed to get back to work, that I needed to focus. I knew what I had to do, but I couldn't seem to get my body to do it.

"Yes, Sir," I said, forcing my mind to function.

"Go with Investigator Cole. We have this."

That was not what I had expected. I thought for sure he was going to lecture me about getting distracted while on a scene. The look on his face though, told me he knew exactly what I was feeling. He knew himself how it felt to have a loved one injured and being taken to the hospital.

I didn't think anyone had noticed the difference between Tristan and I. I thought we had covered up our budding relationship pretty well. Apparently, the one conversation we shared with Captain Clarke had given him more insight into our connection than I had expected.

I really shouldn't have been so surprised that he had noticed something, though. The Captain had always been observant. He had always been able to notice the smallest details. It was what made him so talented out in the field. Of course he would have noticed something in his office earlier. It could have been something simple like a lingering glance that I sent Tristan's way and that was all he needed to know. Still, I wasn't about to look a gift horse in the mouth with this one.

"Thank you, Sir," I promptly shouted back as I climbed into the back of the ambulance just before Newt's partner closed the back doors.

I sat off to the side, doing my best to not get in Newt's way as he worked on Tristan and got his vitals. I watched as he cut up the middle of Tristan's shirt and I was pleased to see there weren't any bruises or burns to his torso. I didn't see any injuries anywhere, so hopefully that meant Taye didn't hurt him before he tied him to that chair. I suspected that Taye might have used Detective West against Tristan to keep him compliant.

What wasn't clear was where Wilson was. If he was still out there, he could be a danger to Tristan. Hopefully, Detective West would be okay and he would be able to find Wilson and get him in cuffs before he decided to go after Tristan. I had no idea if he would come for Tristan, but I had to imagine the man would be upset that his apprentice was now going to prison.

There was no way Taye would be able to talk his way out of it, thankfully. He was going to prison and that meant that Wilson would no longer be able to get his fire jollies out through Taye. He was going to need a new apprentice and it would take time to find one and train them. What I did know for certain was I was not leaving Tristan's side until I knew he would be all right.

The second we arrived at the hospital the back doors of the ambulance were flung open and two doctors were standing there ready and waiting for us. I knew Newt or his partner would have radioed in that they were bringing in a first responder. Even though Tristan was a fire investigator, that still made him a first responder. He was still out on the street every day helping people.

They pulled the stretcher out and started to head inside at a rapid pace. The words started to blur together as Newt spoke what sounded like a different language to give the doctors Tristan's vitals and stats. I didn't really understand most of it, but the doctors' faces didn't change drastically and I took that as a good sign that his vitals weren't too bad. They wheeled him into an exam room, and I started to follow but that was when a nurse stood in front of me to block me from entering the room.

"I'm sorry, Sir, but you have to wait in the waiting room," she said with a warm, but firm smile.

I'd known it was coming, but I hadn't been ready for it. I wanted to be in there with him. I wanted to keep my eyes on him and make sure he was going to be okay. I didn't want to let him out of my sight for a moment but I knew I had to. I had to let the doctors do their job and trust everything would be okay.

"He was in a fire twenty-one years ago. I don't know if that will affect his lungs this time around."

"I will let the doctors know. Do you know if he has asthma or any lasting effects from the first fire?"

"No, he's never said anything and he doesn't have asthma." I was confident on the asthma. In order to be in the Fire Department, to go through the Fire Academy, you couldn't have asthma. The smoke would constantly cause the asthma to act up.

"Thank you, please go and wait in the waiting room. We have your friend."

I had no choice. I gave the nurse a distracted nod and moved away from the room that held Tristan. I had to walk away from the man I was falling in love with as he lay, still unconscious and now hooked up to all kinds of lines and wires, on the stretcher, and with each step that I took away from him I felt a knife stabbing me in my heart. I didn't want to be away from him and now I was going to be stuck in a waiting room for who knew how long.

With a sigh, I stared down at the black plastic chair, but I couldn't bring myself to sit in it. Another ambulance pulled in and I watched as multiple cop cars came with it. I kept my gaze on the ambulance to see if it was Detective West or Taye. I was relieved when they rolled out Detective West and immediately took him into an exam room.

I didn't want it to be Taye, because then he might die from the smoke he'd inhaled and that was too quick of a death for him. He deserved to be trapped in a cell for the rest of his natural life. Based on the look of the cops' faces, they felt the same way. They all piled into the room and flopped into chairs, knowing that it might take a bit before they got any information.

I knew soon enough the waiting room was going to be filled with police and fire fighters as we all showed our support and waited to hear that our men were going to be okay. I just prayed that they both would be.

***

Three hours. It had been three hours and we still didn't know anything about either of them. I knew that wasn't a good sign. Tests could take a while, but it was never good when no one came out to update us. Everyone in the ER knew that there were cops and firefighters flooding the waiting room and the hallways waiting for news on our men.

Captain Amaro was there, but he was keeping further away from everyone. I could see the guilt set on his face. He clearly blamed himself for what his brother had done and I knew it was going to take him a very long time to overcome that feeling of responsibility.

I could also see the looks that some of the other firefighters were giving him. By now, word had spread about Taye and what he had done. They were going to judge Captain Amaro for it, even if that wasn't fair.

The fire department was like high school when it came to gossip and juicy news. It was going to spread faster than an inferno with an accelerant and I wasn't certain that the Captain would survive the blaze. I hoped he would, though. I didn't really know him, but he seemed like a good man. He was obviously brave and cared about his men for him to risk the stares and potential conflict from both firefighters and cops by coming here. The whole situation was a mess and I really had no idea how it was all going to play out. All I could do was be there for Tristan and help get him through it.

"Hawke Colton?" A male voice said off to my left, startling me out of my musing.

I glanced up and saw a man that I did not recognize. He gave me a small, polite smile as he helped himself to the hard plastic chair next to me. I wasn't certain who he was, but I suspected he was a cop. Maybe he had news about Wilson or Taye.

"That's me. Who are you?"

"Mason Wright. I'm a Federal Agent with the Federal Protection Agency."

Now I knew who he was. He was in charge of the FPA, an agency that focused on crimes against children all over the country. They were very popular there in town and I knew that they had helped hundreds of children. They were as close to superheroes as you could get.

"Agent Wright, it's a pleasure to meet you. What can I do for you?" I didn't know why he was here, but I was more than happy to help him.

"Detective West works very closely with us. He's helped us on multiple cases over the years. When I heard that he was in the fire, I started to pull his file to see what he was working on. I went down to the scene and the body of Wilson Stan has been identified. He was in the fire, and based on what your Captain discovered, it looks like Taye shot him and then used him to start the fire. I had my men search Mr. Stan's home and they discovered he had a storage locker. They searched it and they found extensive evidence of the many fires he had started over several years, including proof that he was the one to start the fire twenty-one years ago that killed Investigator Cole's parents. It looks like he started fifty-three fires over the past twenty-five years. He also had a list of potential mentees that he was going to use to start more fires."

Oh my God.

I let out a deep breath I hadn't even realized I'd been holding. I was relieved to hear that Wilson was dead, that was one less threat against Tristan. But to hear that he had started fifty-three fires, that surprised me. We didn't know about that many. We'd thought it was thirty-seven over the past twenty-five years.

And if Wilson had that many fires under his belt, how many did Taye start that we didn't know about?

The whole situation was a mess already and the information Agent Wright had just imparted made things even worse than I'd ever expected. The Investigation Unit would have to go through multiple cases that had been closed as accidental and re-open, re-investigate them and/or change them to arson. They might have to inform surviving victims that they were, in fact, victims to arson. Definitely a mess they would have to wade through, and that was just for Wilson's fires and not

Taye's. They would also have to investigate to make sure that Wilson didn't have another mentee out there.

"That's more fires than we thought. I appreciate your help on the case. I'm sorry about Detective West."

"It's not your fault. He was doing his job and Jonah is far too stubborn to die. He'll be okay. Our tech specialist, Cooper, is going through the federal database to make sure that the electrical device hasn't been used elsewhere. I don't suspect it will have been, but he's going to double check. He's the man with the laptop over there. Him and Jonah are engaged," he said with a nod at a blond haired man who sat in the corner huddled over a laptop and typing furiously.

I had no idea that Detective West was

even with someone. Now I felt terrible, because the man who was in love with Detective West was sitting in a hospital waiting room hoping to hear that he wouldn't have to bury the man that he loved. And yet, he sat there working away on his laptop like he was sitting in a coffee shop.

I wasn't judging. If I could be working right now I would be. It would at least give me something to be distracted by. It hated waiting. I was usually pretty tolerant, but waiting in a hospital to hear about the welfare of people I cared about, there was no amount of patience in the world to get me through that.

Before I could say anything else, a doctor finally came out from behind the double doors to the ER bays. I didn't get up. I held my breath and waited to see if he was here for Detective West or for Tristan. Before he even spoke he had everyone's attention by just walking into the room.

"Good evening, everyone. I have an update on both of your men brought in today," the doctor started and now I stood up. We all made our way over to the doctor so we could hear everything the man said.

"Detective West was given oxygen and taken for a CT-Scan for his head. He has a concussion, but he has regained consciousness and is currently on oxygen to help with the smoke inhalation. He will make a full recovery and he can leave in a few days. We need to monitor his lungs and his concussion, but we suspect that no additional problems will arise. He should be able to be back on the street within two months."

Everyone clapped and I saw some of the police officers give Cooper a hug or a pat on his shoulder. I could see the relief on his face and I couldn't blame the man. I wanted that relief, too, and I prayed that the doctor wasn't giving us the good news first and saving the bad news for last.

"Investigator Cole didn't sustain any physical injuries outside of some bruising and abrasions to his wrists. He sustained more smoke inhalation than Detective West, but that was to be expected with him being higher than Detective West. He is on a ventilator currently and he will need to be on it for a few days to help his lungs heal. We suspect that he, too, will make a full recovery and he should be able to go home in seven days, assuming his lungs start to heal properly, which I believe they will. He will have to take it slow for the next three to six months, and he will have to go through breathing treatments and exercises, but I am confident that his lungs will mend and he will be able to return to work."

I closed my eyes and felt a rush at the pure relief that flooded my body. Tristan was going to be okay. I hated that he was hooked up to a ventilator, of course, but I understood the need to give his lungs a break. The only thing that mattered was that he would recover. It might be a bit of a long journey, but I would be there for him through it all.

"Can I see him?" I asked.

"Yes, of course. One person at a time

right now, both Investigator Cole and Detective West need to rest. Investigator Cole is in room four-ten and Detective West is in room two-fifteen."

"Thank you so much, Doctor," I said, flashing him a warm smile.

The doctor gave a nod and then he headed off, getting patted on the shoulder by both cops and firefighters.

I didn't even wait around for anyone to say anything to me. I had to get to Tristan and see him with my own eyes. He didn't have family and he didn't really have any friends. All he had was me and I would make damn sure he didn't wake up alone this time. This time around, when he woke up I would be sitting there with him. He was going to wake up knowing that he wasn't alone and someone was there who cared about him.

As I walked into his hospital room though, I was not prepared to see him lying so still. I was not prepared to see him with the ventilator pumping air into his lungs and helping him breathe. I knew he was hooked up to it, and I knew it was giving his lungs the break they needed so they could heal, but that didn't make the sight any easier to handle.

I slowly made my way over to the bed, watching Tristan's eyes for any movement, though I really didn't expect any. I bent forward and placed a gentle kiss on his forehead. I pulled the chair over so it was closer to the side of the bed before I sat down. I threaded my fingers through his on the one hand closest to me and then moved my right hand his head and ran my fingertips through his hair.

I had to fight to keep my anger down at the sight of the black and blue of bruises that wrapped around both of his wrists. I would have loved five minutes alone with Taye for everything he had done to Tristan. I would have loved to make sure he knew exactly what pain was. I couldn't, though, and I would have no choice but to wait for the day he was sentenced to life in prison.

I knew the investigation into Taye was only just beginning. It wouldn't surprise me if another agency took over the case with the close connection to Captain Amaro. Tristan wouldn't want to let it go, but he might not have much of a choice with having to be on medical leave for the next few months.

Regardless, we would get through it. He wasn't alone in this world anymore and I would do everything to make sure he knew it.

"I'm right here, Darlin', for when you are ready to wake up." And that was a promise I would always keep.

EPILOGUE

Three Months Later...

Tristan

LEANING AGAINST THE railing, I enjoyed the view as the sun almost completely disappeared off in the distance, leaving behind shades of crimson, burnt orange, and butter yellow. I still couldn't believe this was my view. I couldn't believe I'd managed to accomplish it. It might not seem like much to most people, but to me it was everything.

I had bought a house, *a real house*, that I was planning on turning into a home. The first home that I'd had since my parents were killed. It was a huge step for me and I was terrified to make it. I had gone to look at close to a hundred houses for sale over the last three months. None of them had felt *right* and the ones that did feel good, I had been too afraid to make the jump.

Hawke had been amazing with me. He came and looked at every single house with me. He didn't judge me when I turned them all down. He didn't get annoyed when I refused to pick a house. He just reassured me that I would know which one was my home when I walked into it. I thought he was crazy, but then we saw this house and I felt it.

I truly *felt it.*

The place instantly felt like home and I knew before even seeing the whole house that I had to have it.

It was a three bedroom home, not that I needed more than one bedroom, but I was open to fostering and the extra bedrooms would be nice for that. It had all been renovated recently so I didn't have to do anything to it. It was an open concept home and I liked that I could see the kitchen and living room completely. The kitchen was beautiful with clean with white cabinets and countertops. There was an island that faced the living room with enough room for four bar stools. I knew right away that island was a place that I would be spending a lot of time at for meals and working.

One of the best features of the house was the working fireplace that required real wood. We had one growing up at my parents' house and I'd loved it. We used to cook hotdogs on it or make s'mores and drink hot chocolate. I had a lot of great memories from the hours we'd spent in front of the fire and I wanted to that continue tradition again. I wanted to be able to share that with the children that I would eventually bring into my home.

The backyard was also very impressive. I had two acres of property and it would be perfect for a garden, having a little playground, and I was thinking of having an above ground pool. I was also thinking about getting a dog.

I'd never had one growing up because my mom was allergic to pet hair. I'd never had one when I was with my grandparents, because they always wanted everything spotless. I knew this would be a perfect chance to have the dog I'd always dreamed of having.

I looked forward to having a real life again. To make this house a home and go back to living.

A smile instantly turned up the corners of my mouth as I felt strong arms wrap around my waist. Hawke pressed his warm lips on my cheek before he spoke.

"How are you feeling? Lungs tight?"

I had to fight not to roll my eyes. It had been a very common recurring question from Hawke for months. I understood why he was worried. I did.

He had found me barely alive in the middle of a fire. This time around I had been lucky to avoid getting burned, but only because he had arrived in time to save my ass and Detective West's.

I did, however, inhale a nasty amount of smoke, resulting in me being hooked up to a ventilator for a week and in the hospital for two more weeks after that.

Hawke had been amazing through it all. He spent every day and night with me the whole time I was there. Captain Clarke had allowed him to take the time off without a single complaint. The man was very generous and he understood what was going on without Hawke needing to say anything.

When I did finally get to leave the hospital, they'd discharged me with a prescription for an inhaler for when my chest got tight or I just couldn't catch my breath quite right. I didn't have asthma, but with the smoke inhalation, I was still going to have moments where I needed the inhaler until my lungs were fully healed. Right after I'd left the hospital, I'd had to use it a few times a day, but in the past couple of weeks I hadn't needed it at all. That still didn't change the fact that Hawke worried about me.

"I'm fine. It's been two weeks since I've used the inhaler. I have even been able to go for runs again. I'm good, Babe."

"Good. Why don't we test that fireplace out? We can sit on a blanket and enjoy a drink with the fire going," he suggested.

"Sounds perfect."

"All right, I'll get the fire started. Why don't you grab us a blanket and we can relax."

"Sounds good. Do you want wine or whiskey?"

"Whichever you're feeling. I'm not picky," he said with a small shrug before he pulled away from me and strolled over to where the wood was kept. There wasn't too much left from the previous owner and I knew I would have to get some before the winter months hit. It didn't get very cold there, but the nights could be chilly and it would be nice to warm up the house with a fire.

I made my way inside and upstairs to grab a blanket. I had moved in yesterday, but I hadn't done much in the way of unpacking outside of the kitchen. I didn't have much to unpack. I had to order furniture and have it delivered to even have much in my house. I did order a new bed though, and I was very happy about that. I hadn't realized how uncomfortable my bed had been until I'd slept on my new one last night. I hadn't slept that well in decades, though it definitely helped that Hawke held me all night long.

I grabbed a thick blanket and made my way back down the stairs. I spread it out on the floor, tossing down a couple of couch cushions, too, as Hawke worked away at getting the fire going. I went over and poured us both two fingers of whiskey over ice in crystal glasses. I didn't mind wine, but I wasn't feeling like it tonight.

I placed the glasses down on the side table just as Hawke stood from where he kneeled by the fireplace. With a grin, he went and sat down with his back against the fat cushions and I plopped down in front of him with my back pressed against his chest. His arms wrapped around me, pulling me into his body heat, and just like that I felt relaxed and at home.

"You know, I love what we do in the bedroom, but I love this part too," I admitted.

The time we spent in the bedroom was incredible; it was earth shattering and eye opening, no doubt about it, but I did love these moments, too. The moments where it was just us and we could relax and enjoy each other's company. We didn't need to talk or even have to watch anything. We could just curl up with each other and enjoy having the other near. I felt him press his lips the side of my head before he spoke, echoing exactly what I had been thinking.

"It's these moments, the lazy days in bed, waking up in each other's arms, those are the moments that make a relationship for me. It's more than just sex, even though the sex is definitely very good and important, too."

"Oh, it's very good," I said, with a flirty smile plastered on my face as I turned my head to look at him. I leisurely ran my hand up Hawke's inner thigh to his already half-hard dick. "Very good, indeed."

Hawke let out a soft moan before he grabbed me and turned me around so I was straddling his lap. He slowly closed the gap between us and gently pressed his lips against my own. The kiss was soft and slow, but it was filled with passion. Hawke had a way of taking even the most simplest of kisses and making me feel loved and wanted. The passion and desire he could put into a kiss was remarkable and I never wanted to stop kissing him.

I felt his tongue lightly licking at my bottom lip, requesting permission, and I happily opened my mouth and welcomed the addition of his tongue. I couldn't help the whimper that slipped from my lips at the feel of his tongue dancing with mine as he deepened the kiss.

He placed one of his hands on the back of my neck and ran the other down my back to cup my ass. He squeezed a cheek and the movement caused my hips to rock forward, rubbing our hard, cloth-covered dicks against each other. We both began to pant, little moans and groans escaping us as I continued to rock my hips and grind myself against him.

It amazed me how strong my desire was for him, and his for me. We had been having sex for months now, and I figured our desire for each other, our *need* for each other, would have cooled off by now. Only it hadn't. No matter how many times we'd had sex, we'd never lost that uncontrollable need for the other person. Our desire continued to rage, soaring to levels I'd never experienced before in my life with any other man. Our cravings for one another were just as scorching hot and exhilarating as the first time we'd been intimate and I highly doubt that would ever change.

When the need to breathe became too much, Hawke pulled back and started to pepper kisses down my neck as I continued to rock our hips together. My own hands instinctively went to the hem of Hawke's shirt and I started to pull it up his chest.

I needed to feel his delicious bare skin against mine in the worst way.

Tugging it off over his head, I quickly divested him of his shirt and Hawke did the same with mine. With our shirts out of the way, I could run my hands down his chest and enjoy the feel of his toned abs, play with the fine hair on his happy trail, but it was nowhere near enough for either of us. The pleasure was blazing through us and we had yet to even truly touch.

Getting the rest of our clothes off would be tricky; neither one of us wanted to break contact with the other and I definitely did not want to get up. I worked swiftly on undoing his pants as his hands fumbled with my belt. I sat up slightly so Hawke could lift his hips and I was able to slide his pants and boxers off of him.

Once we had him naked, I sat up on my knees and removed one leg of my pants at a time. With my pants and boxers removed, I dropped back down onto his lap and rocked my hips against his. The second the bare skin of our hard cocks touched directly, we both let out a deep moan in unison.

"Hawke..."

"That's it, Darlin', just feel," he whispered into my ear before he gently nibbled on the lobe.

I moaned as I continued to rock my hips slowly, letting our pleasure build. Hawke's lips were back on mine, his kiss deep as his hands moved up and down my back and over my ass. I took the time to run my own hands over his chest and stomach, exploring every inch of his body, feeling every bump and groove as my fingers danced over his skin. Our need was increasing slowly, building up the volcano within us.

It was Hawke who broke first, needing more contact than the slow rhythmic rocking that I had been doing. He placed his hand on my lower back and gently rolled us over, pulling me underneath him on the soft, thick blanket. I opened my legs so he could fit between them as he pressed his hand down my body to my ass and ground himself against me. He kissed all along my neck and over my chest, nibbling one hard nipple and then the other as he continued to grind his cock against mine, frotting and fueling the inferno inside of me.

"I need to be inside of you," Hawke whispered against the hollow at the base of my neck, scraping his five o'clock shadow over my collarbone. I knew the delectable marks he left there would be a scrumptious reminder in the morning.

"Fuck, yes, please," I whined as a shockwave of electrical pleasure shot up my spine and I arched my back.

Hawke sat up on his knees and I immediately followed, wrapping my mouth around his swollen tip. Hawke hissed at the unexpected pleasure. I knew he had intended to reach for the lube, but I wasn't about to let him get away from me that easily.

I took him down to his base with a deep moan as his dick slid along my tongue and his flavor exploded in my mouth. Hawke started to lightly thrust in my mouth, his hand going to my hair to hold my head in place, and I couldn't stop moaning my appreciation. The small submissive part of me loved it when he did that.

I loved knowing that I could push him to the edge of bliss, to drive him wild with his need to feel more. He never went too far or too hard. He made sure he didn't cause me to choke or hurt me. He was always in control, even at the height of his pleasure.

I could feel him getting harder and I

knew he was close. I moaned again, long and low, knowing it would send vibrations straight down his dick.

Hawke let out a cry, shouting my name as he snapped his hips forward and came hard down my throat. I greedily sucked and swallowed everything he had for me as his breaths shuttled from his chest.

He was still half-hard and I continued to suck on him until I felt his dick grow once again. With a final suck to his tip, I popped my mouth off his cock and lifted my head and at once his mouth crashed down over mine, his lips capturing mine. His tongue invaded my welcoming mouth as he carefully pushed me back down onto the blanket.

He effortlessly slipped between my legs as I heard him opening the lube bottle that he had managed to reach. His mouth never left mine as he teased my pucker for a moment, just long enough to make me buck my hips with need, before he inserted his fingers inside of my hole. I whimpered into the kiss and I couldn't help but rock my hips to get more friction and encourage him deeper.

Our mutual need was reaching a peak and once Hawke felt that I was stretched enough, he removed his fingers from inside me and once again switched our positions so I was straddling his lap, the balls of my feet perched on the thick blanket, heels in the air, as he sat back against the couch.

"Go slow, let it build up, Darlin'."

The last thing I wanted to do was to go slow, but I understood what he wanted. He didn't want to rush this one, like so many times before. He wanted both of us to experience new heights of pleasure and I was all for it.

I lowered myself down onto the tip of his dick. I went slow, and bit by bit, took all of his girthy hardness until he was balls deep and I sat on his hips, both of us breathing heavily. It was glorious to be able to feel him inside of me once again. I was never going to get tired of feeling his dick buried inside of me.

"You feel so good. Your body was meant for me and mine was meant for you." He kissed all along my neck as he spoke, his whiskey-scented breath feathering over my skin in little puffs of cool air, and I could feel goosebumps rise over my hot skin in his wake.

I couldn't argue with that at all. I

knew we had both felt it before, that familiarity to the other. As if we had loved each other for several past life times and once again our bodies were reconnecting, our souls were reconnecting, merging as we came together once more as one.

I let out a breathy moan as I leisurely slid myself upward until I was almost at his tip before I slowly moved back down with a hiss, enjoying the stretch and burn in my channel as his thick cock filled me in all the right ways. I continued to go agonizingly slow just like he wanted. The pace was driving me insane but his pleasure was my top priority and I knew it would be worth it in the end.

He placed his hands on my hips, grasping them to force me to keep the unhurried pace. He already knew once I hit my sweet spot it would be hard for me to keep the pace slow.

I angled my hips so I could hit my sweet spot and I let out a loud cry the second his dick hit it dead on.

Hawke held onto my hips tighter, his fingers digging into my skin as my need to go faster increased. I knew I'd have bruises there tomorrow but I didn't care.

"Go slow, Darlin'. I want to watch as you come all over my belly without me even touching your dick."

I moaned as I put my head back and arched slightly so the angle would be even better. Hawke kissed and nipped at my neck, lightly thrusting into me to make himself go even deeper inside of me. We were both moaning, our bodies trembling with need, but we continued to move leisurely as one.

I wrapped my arms around Hawke's neck as he held me close against his chest. We kissed slowly and gently, just as our movements were. We allowed our bodies to feel everything that the other was giving to it without the need to chase our pleasure. It built slowly and I truly felt amazing. I had no idea that sex could ever feel this wonderful. It was always amazing with Hawke, but this felt on a whole other level. This wasn't sex, this was tender love making, as if our souls were physically connecting to the other. It was overwhelming and remarkable all at the same time.

Time held no meaning. I couldn't tell if it had been ten minutes or ten hours that we had been pleasuring each other in slow motion. I just knew it was excruciating and incredible all at once, my pleasure centers were firing at top speed, I felt almost high from the endorphins flooding my system, and I never wanted this moment to end.

I felt the heat in the pit of my stomach turn into an inferno and my balls pulled up tight. My panting and moans had picked up and I felt like I was about to explode. I could feel Hawke getting even harder within me and I knew he was close, too. I couldn't stop moaning as my walls tightened around his cock and my body detonated.

The tightening of my walls was enough to push Hawke over the edge and he erupted fiercely inside of me. I couldn't contain the deep moan at the heat from his jizz filling the inside of me, scorching my walls.

"Hawke," I moaned as it felt like my whole body became consumed with his heat. I felt complete at the very simple sensation. As if there was a piece of Hawke within me, a part of his soul that would forever belong to me now.

Once I finally stopped pulsing, I placed my forehead against his as we both tried to catch our breath. I felt lightheaded and my body was weak and trembling from the pleasure and exertion. At the same time, I felt a bit like I would never again catch my breath, like I floated, a bit stoned. I knew it was from all of the panting and lack of oxygen, but I didn't care. I loved the heavenly euphoric feeling and I never wanted to come back down to earth.

Hawke pulled me in for a gentle kiss before he pulled back. He too was breathing heavily and seemed like he barely had enough oxygen himself. Still, he placed a hand on the side of my face, cupping my cheek in his meaty palm as he spoke with so much love and emotion lacing his voice that it nearly brought tears to my eyes.

"I love you."

Those were three words I never thought I would ever hear again. I never expected to ever fall in love with someone, nor had I wanted to. I had been fully prepared to handle life completely alone, baggage and all, and I had been good with that. And then Hawke came into my life and completely destroyed my world. He blew it up without a single care or concern for the consequences as he tore down all my carefully built up walls and I should probably hate him for it, but I loved him. He had saved me, even when I didn't know I needed saving. He was my soulmate and I was his.

"I love you, too."

Hawke pulled me to him once more, his mouth capturing mine in a tender but passionate kiss. He kept it slow, but I could feel exactly how much he loved me through that single kiss.

I let out a soft moan and melted into his arms. After a moment, Hawke placed his hand on the small of my back and flipped us once again so I was lying back down on the blanket with Hawke now above me. Hawke slowly moved his hips back and forth as he softly began to fuck me once more.

I broke the kiss first as I couldn't help but pant heavily, my heart tripping at the pleasure already slowly building inside of me yet again.

"I'm going to make love to you all night, Darlin'."

I could hear the promise in his voice and it was one I knew I was going to thoroughly enjoy. Suddenly, I was no longer tired and in need of a breather. I felt energized and ready for Hawke to fulfill his pledge.

This night was going to be special and I knew I would always remember it for the rest of my life. Just like I knew that tonight was only one of the many nights that Hawke and I would share together. For the first time in decades, I couldn't wait to see what the future had in store for me.

Thank you for reading!

EVIE RILEY

Continue the series with <u>Cyrus</u>, Book
Two in Smokejumpers.

OTHER BOOKS BY EVIE

Federal Protection Agency
Mason
Rafe
Ryzen
Cooper
Noah
Damien
Sebastian
Gabe
Logan

Ruthless Empire
Courting Danger
Chasing Danger
Kissing Danger

Smokejumpers
Hawke
Cyrus
Jase
Gage
Jackson
Xavier

Jasper Springs
Cade
Dawson
Drew
Grayson
Riley
Mitch

From The Edge
Shattered
Runaway
Jaded
Rescue
Hidden
Tormented

Gray Vale Pack
His Fated Mate
His Wounded Warrior
His Healing Heart

ABOUT THE AUTHOR

Evie Riley is a prolific, neurodivergent author known for her captivating MM romance novels. She has gained a significant following and topped the LGBT+ action and adventure bestseller charts with her series.

Evie's writing style often explores dark and gritty themes where her men must overcome difficult obstacles in their search for love, but she has also ventured into sweeter small-town romances, incorporating tropes like enemies-to-lovers, friends-to-lovers, age-gap, and forced proximity. She is known for crafting engaging romantic suspense novels and has a knack for creating interconnected series worlds that keep readers invested.

Interestingly, Ms. Riley has hinted at exploring new genres, such as Alien Omegaverse Romance, in the future.

Outside of writing, she enjoys spending time at the beach and has a quirky personality, described by her partner as ranging from cute to deadly, depending on her blood-chocolate levels.

Evie spends her nights writing bad boys in love, and her days wrangling the sweet boys she loves.